THE TRENCH

PAUL MANNERING

SEVERED PRESS
HOBART TASMANIA

THE TRENCH

CHAPTER 1

The coffee tasted worse than bitter, as if the water had gone sour. Michael sipped the cold brew anyway. So far, the flight from Honolulu to Auckland on a US Navy C-130 Hercules had been long and dull. It got colder as they headed south. New Zealand was as close to Antarctica as Michael ever wanted to get. A great place for skiing in winter, but he preferred water-skiing and surfing in tropical Hawaii.

Trying to sleep in the vibrating hold of the cargo plane proved impossible. The facilities were Spartan, and Michael thought the coffee might have been recycled from the airplane's chemical toilet. The only food provided were MRE ration packs, and they tasted worse than the coffee.

Lying on his back, his eyes closed, arms tucked into his jacket, Michael replayed recent events in his head. After a long night of tequila shots and passion, he had finally fallen asleep with a surfer girl wrapped around him, all salt scent and hard muscle. Her name had been Niki, or Viki or something. He woke up when the pounding in his head had been drowned out by a steady knocking on the door of the hotel room.

Eyes half-closed, Michael opened the door. A man in a crisp khaki US Navy Ensign's uniform and precision haircut stood before him and regarded Michael with professional blankness.

A woman with a lieutenant's insignia on her uniform stood to one side.

"Yeah?" Michael said through the mold growing on his tongue.

"Doctor Saint-Clair?" the Ensign asked.

"Ah... no??" Michael replied.

"Would you mind stepping aside, sir?"

"What is this all about?"

"Sir, I have orders to collect Doctor Nicole Saint-Clair from this location."

"I have no idea who–Wait, this isn't my hotel room."

The ensign stepped forward and entered the suite. With a casual sweep of the room, he took in the empty bottles and the discarded clothes.

The lieutenant stepped into the room, her hands clasped behind her back in a formal gesture. She studied Michael intently for a moment. "Are you Michael Armitage?" she asked.

"Who wants to know?"

"The United States Government."

"What is this about?"

"I recognize you from the photo Lieutenant Armitage keeps on her locker door."

"You're here to blackmail me or something?"

"Of course, not. What you do in your life is none of my concern. You might want to talk to your wife though."

"Ex-wife. I mean, we're separated." Michael pinched the bridge of his nose. "It's complicated. Now if you'll excuse me, I appear to be in the wrong hotel room." Michael stumbled back towards the bedroom and then paused, "Uhh, help yourselves to a drink."

The blonde woman sat up when he walked in, a sheet demurely clasped against her chest, the tanned curve of her back all bared and perfect.

"Who you talking to?"

"Someone looking for Nicole Saint-Clair." Michael avoided eye contact and scooped up his jeans, sneakers, and shirt from the floor.

"Who? The police?"

"US Navy, ma'am." The female lieutenant stood in the bedroom doorway.

Michael took the opportunity to slip into the ensuite bathroom. He washed his face and took a long look at himself. Unshaven, on the wrong side of thirty, and on the last month of his credit cards. He wondered how bad his luck had to be if his wife's shipmates turned up in the hotel room of some woman he had hooked up with.

Dressed and awake, he returned to the bedroom and stopped, Nicole was pulling on clothes while the female lieutenant stood by.

"Hey, she's got nothing to do with this, uhh, whatever this is."

"You can wait in the other room, Mister Armitage," the lieutenant said.

Michael blinked and then stumbled into the living room. He found sunglasses and the room keys for a different hotel on the coffee table. "Mind telling me what this is all about?"

"I am not at liberty to say, sir." The ensign hadn't moved.

"I was pretty drunk last night, maybe I pissed off you and your buddies?"

"I don't drink, sir."

"Neither do I. At least, never again."

"Let's go, Ensign," the lieutenant said, emerging from the bedroom, Nicole following in her wake, wearing jeans, boots and a surfer T-shirt. A backpack was slung over her shoulder.

"Thanks for last night, Michael," Nicole said as she walked past.

"Sure, sorry about the early wake up." Michael shrugged apologetically.

"Not your fault."

"After you, sir." The ensign fell into step behind Michael and closed the door on the way out.

Descending the stairs, Michael pushed his hands into his jeans pockets. His wedding ring felt cold, and he slipped it on his finger like Frodo with the One Ring.

They emerged into the glorious morning of a Hawaiian spring day. At the street side, the ensign opened the rear passenger door on a non-descript SUV with dark, tinted windows. Nicole and the lieutenant got in. Michael stopped.

"Well, I guess I'll be on my way then."

"One moment please, sir." The ensign leaned down and listened to someone hidden in the shadow of the vehicle's interior.

"Doctor Armitage, we would like to offer you a ride," he said, straightening up.

"It's okay. My hotel is two blocks that way. I can walk."

"Get in the car, sir."

"Not without some explanation."

"I am not at liberty to discuss that with you, sir." The ensign's hand dropped to the holstered pistol on his hip. Michael found the gesture more chilling than the stone-faced refusal to answer his questions.

"For someone whose job it is to defend America's freedom, you sure don't have a lot of it yourself."

"I do just fine, sir."

Michael stared at the gun for a moment then followed the man's gesture to get in the car.

"What is going on?" Nicole asked.

"I'm going for a ride. You?"

"Same. Did they tell you what this was about?"

"Not in so many words."

"Not at liberty to say?"

"Something like that."

"You must have really pissed someone off last night."

"I don't remember much about last night," Michael admitted.

Nicole regarded him steadily. "You approached me at the hotel bar, declared that you were a free-diving world champion and you could go deeper, longer, and harder than any man alive."

"I did?"

"That was just your opening line. Then you proceeded to try and buy me drinks."

"Tequila…" Michael felt the taste of it in his throat even now.

"Tequila, bourbon, and vodka shots. You then tried to explain the biochemistry of intoxication."

"Did I make any sense?"

"To someone with no idea what you were talking about, sure. You did get your secondary and tertiary ethanol metabolism pathways confused. Then you got stuck pronouncing dehydrogenase."

"Nicole Saint-Clair…? You gave the lecture about molecular

evolution at the conference?"

"I'm touched you remembered."

"I saw your name on the program. I didn't actually attend the lecture."

"That's a shame. You might have learned something."

"Marine biology is my field. Particularly hydrozoans."

"I know. You told me last night. Of course, by that point you couldn't say hydrozoan. Let alone jellyfish. But I guessed."

"Michael Armitage," Michael extended a hand.

"Nicole, Nicole Saint-Clair."

"Did we–?"

"Oh yeah, though you were almost unconscious by the third time."

The lieutenant got behind the wheel, next to the unseen passenger. The ensign took the window seat next to Michael in the back.

Michael curled his hands into fists and worked his wedding ring in a circle as the SUV pulled out into the Honolulu traffic. Gretchen had always put her career first, though to be fair, Michael's research had been his focus since they met.

"You weren't wearing that wedding ring last night." Nicole's bright tone had an artificial twang to it.

"It's complicated." Michael resisted the urge to sit on his hand.

"Separated? Divorced?"

"Gretchen is away with work a lot."

"You're married and your wife's name is Gretchen." Nicole's jaw went tight and she turned to stare out the window.

"Gretchen Armitage is a lieutenant in the US Navy," the

woman driving said.

"Oh God…" Nicole reddened. "I have never done anything like that before."

"Quite the coincidence." The male passenger in the front seat wore a suit and sunglasses. From behind him, where Michael sat, he looked close to retirement. Though, that didn't mean much in government circles. The guy sounded educated, calm, and in control. Someone who was used to being listened to without ever having to raise his voice.

"It's embarrassing," Nicole muttered.

"Get over it," the man in the suit replied. "Coincidences are nothing more than mistakes with fortunate outcomes."

"I think I have had that fortune cookie before," Michael said.

"In this instance, Doctor Armitage, we required two experts in specialist fields. The fortunate coincidence for us was that two of them were in the same hotel room this morning. Doctor Kurt Ramaldi was my first choice."

"Ramaldi? Seriously?"

"He has produced some of the most well-received papers in his field of the last five years."

"Ramaldi's work is all theoretical. None of his conclusions hold up in a natural environment. He works entirely in computer modelling."

"His presentation at the conference was interesting, or did you miss that one too?" Nicole asked and went back to staring at the passing traffic.

Michael gave a disgusted snort. "Ramaldi applies perfect parameters to his experiments and then has the audacity to say it proves exactly what he wants it to prove."

"You do not believe that computer modelling has any place in biological research?" the man in the front seat asked.

"Sure it does, just not Ramaldi's computer modelling."

"He's right," Nicole spoke up. "Ramaldi's work looks good, but his data is flawed."

"The often vaunted, but never sought, second opinion," the passenger said with a nod. "I am sure between the two of you we can have a resolution in no time."

The SUV rolled to a halt at the gate of the US Navy and Air Force joint base, Pearl Harbor-Hickam. After a quick flash of identification from the driver and a cursory eyeball of the civilians in the back, they were waved through.

Michael's stomach tied in knots, anything involving the US military made him nervous. He didn't really subscribe to the whole patriotic salute-the-flag attitude of some of his fellow Americans. On the bright side, there might be some much-needed research funding to come out of this consultancy.

The vehicle drove across the campus, past houses and low office buildings. Men and women in uniform were everywhere and Michael kept double-checking to make sure that Gretchen wasn't one of them. After passing through another security gate, this one bringing them to the dockside area of the base, the SUV stopped.

Michael and Nicole waited until the driver opened the back door and then climbed out.

"This way, sir, ma'am," their escort said, indicating a cinderblock and steel building. The passenger in the suit joined them on the baking concrete. He was Caucasian, his hair close-cropped, his demeanor as government-issued as his suit.

The sailor on guard outside opened the door as they

approached. Inside, the atmosphere was air-conditioned and smelled of careful cleaning.

Entering a conference room, Michael and Nicole took the seats offered around a long table. The ensign went to arrange coffee and breakfast for the visitors. The man in the suit went and closed the blinds on the other side and then stood, staring at the grey slats. The lieutenant closed the door and stayed outside.

"I'm sure you are aware of the limited knowledge we have of the world's oceans," the man in the suit said to the blocked window. "It is quite true that we know more about outer space than we do about the water that makes up seventy percent of the planet."

"Seventy-one percent," Michael said absently. "Ninety-six percent of that water is in the seas and oceans. The rest is lakes, rivers, snow, polar ice, and bottled water."

The man nodded. "I am preaching to the choir." They sat in silence for an awkward moment. "Before we go any further, there is paperwork to sign. Standard non-disclosure agreements." Two slim manila folders were slid across the table to the scientists. Mr. Suit gave them a moment to flick through the multi-page documents.

"Suffice to say, the essence of the dense legalese is that if you communicate anything you witness during your time assisting the US government in this matter, to any person, for any reason, without due authorization, the remaining days of your life will be more unpleasant than you can possibly imagine."

"We don't even know what this is about," Nicole said. "You're threatening us and we don't even know why."

"You are not being threatened, Doctor Saint-Clair, simply

informed."

"We can walk away at any time?" Nicole asked.

"Possibly." The man in the suit turned and regarded them both.

"If this is some kind of consultancy work, how much are we getting paid?" Michael asked.

"Enough to clear your debts and fund your research for at least five years, Doctor Armitage."

"Are we going to end up having to appear before a Congressional sub-committee of inquiry?" Michael asked.

Mr. Suit almost smiled. "I can assure you, Doctor Armitage, *that* will never happen."

The door opened and the ensign entered, bearing a tray of steaming coffees and covered plates of bacon, eggs, and hash browns.

Michael sipped his coffee gratefully, feeling the life flow into his limbs as the pressure eased behind his eyes. The food eased the roiling of his belly, and he and Nicole ate in silence for a few minutes.

When they were done, Mr. Suit laid a pen between the two folders on the table. "Initial each page, then sign at the end."

Michael and Nicole looked at each other and then signed.

CHAPTER 2

Nicole had barely spoken a word since they boarded the plane at Pearl Harbor, and began their long flight south. She just burrowed deeper into the fur-lined jacket she had been issued with and seemed to be asleep.

Michael had laughed when Mr. Suit's presentation finished. The content of it was patently ridiculous. He began with a PowerPoint presentation, old slides still labelled classified, showing drawings and photographs of a serious construction project. To Michael, it looked like an underground bunker, the sort of thing science-fiction writers in the 1950s imagined people living in after the bombs fell in the final war with the Soviet Union.

"The concept of the rock-site was a Cold War initiative. At key locations around the world, underground bases, built-in marine environments, would provide covert operational centers for surveillance of Soviet submarine fleets. In the decades since the Cold War finished, the remaining facilities were either mothballed or re-designated for scientific research."

"What kind of research?" Nicole asked.

"The kind that does not earn the scientists involved a Nobel Prize, or publishing credits in peer-reviewed journals," Mr. Suit said drily. "It does, however, make an invaluable contribution to National Security."

"So, not cures for cancer, HIV, or Ebola then?" Nicole asked.

"The specific nature of the various projects is irrelevant to your involvement."

At this point, Michael got the giggles. "Seriously? You brought us in here to admit that the US Navy built secret underwater bases?"

"It is background information to provide context for what you are about to witness."

The screen flickered and a video recording of a bearded man seated in a cramped laboratory speaking directly into the camera came online. In Michael's professional estimation, he looked like shit.

"I am Doctor Bernard Saul, biological research laboratory head at SUD 8. It's ahh... three in the morning local time. I'm going to record this and transmit it via the secure network."

The man on the video sighed, and rubbed his eyes, pushing his glasses up onto his forehead. "I haven't slept in a couple of days, so I'll try and make sense. There's something... ah... wrong here. I don't know how else to describe the current situation. We've been regular as clockwork with our psych assessments, and you've no doubt seen the reports. The crew here are excellent people. Well trained, professionals in their fields. About a week ago, lab technician, Andrew Filden, went missing. We are a contained environment, so it's not likely he wandered outside and ahh, got lost in the snow." Saul laughed, a thin nasal sound with a sharp edge of hysteria.

"Andy turned up again two days later. He was a little weird, to be honest, but we figured it was just a hangover. Maybe he'd been hitting some home-brewed hooch and went on a bender. Filden was the first. One of the Navy crew was reported missing a day later. He showed up again after twenty-four hours and refused to answer any questions about his absence. The crew chief took care of it. Put him in the brig or whatever it is they do these days."

Saul turned and stared into the darkness beyond the light cast by the computer monitor. "Whatever is ahh… affecting the onsite personnel, is spreading. Observable symptoms are an absence from usual routine or duties. Then within twenty-four hours, the missing person shows up again. But different, you know? I mean, they look the same, but they are kinda shut down. Subdued, less emotional or engaged. I suggested to Doctor Nakiro that she might like to conduct blood tests on everyone. She went missing later that day. When she turned up again, she told me that everything was fine." Saul leaned into the camera. "Everything is not fine. Everything is as fucking far from fine right now as it could possibly be." Saul took a breath and rubbed his eyes.

"I'm worried that this is connected with the Galahad project." Saul paused and shivered. "I am officially notifying you that I have started the countdown timer for the Death Valley Protocol. I really need a reason to terminate the countdown."

A shadow moved in the background, just beyond the edge of the monitor's glow. Saul jerked and stared over his shoulder. Turning back, he said, "If you can send help, be damned caref-"

The video turned to grey static and then went black.

"What is the Death Valley Protocol?" Nicole asked.

"This really sounds like a military issue, not a science problem," Michael said.

"The military solution is under control, Doctor Armitage. The science problem is the one Doctor Saint-Clair and yourself are going to review and report on."

"What is the Death Valley Protocol?" Nicole asked again, her voice raised.

"The DVP is a final solution authorization to sterilize a research facility in the event of a containment breach that poses a significant threat to national security."

"How does it work?" Nicole asked.

"That information is classified and not relevant to your mission, Doctor Saint-Clair."

"If you are asking us to go into a place that may have already been, what, sterilized? I'd say it is highly relevant."

"The protocol was never enacted. A marine security team has entered the site and will resolve any personnel issues before you arrive."

"Hey, if we find a new species of fish, we get to name it, right?" Michael grinned.

CHAPTER 3

Auckland felt distinctly cooler than Honolulu. The humidity under the lead-colored sky was offset by the wind coming in off the ocean, carrying with it the reminder of how much closer to Antarctica they now were.

For the first time in his life, Michael didn't go through immigration or any of the usual processes when entering a foreign country. Instead, a black SUV met them on the tarmac, and they were driven through a suburban city with a strange mix of English colonial and modern South Pacific architecture.

"Devonport Navy Base," the American driver announced. The security was less obvious than they were used to. A quick check of the driver's photographic ID and they were waved through.

Michael and Nicole were allowed twenty minutes to shower, change into heavy-duty survival suits, and eat a hot meal. The SUV then dropped them next to a helicopter that bore no markings of country or military origin.

"Saint-Clair and Armitage?" an American woman in a pilot's jumpsuit and helmet asked.

"Yeah?" Michael replied. Nicole just nodded, her face pale and drawn.

"Ready to go?"

"Uhm, sure?" No one had given them any more information

other than Mr. Suit at his briefing. Michael was still processing everything they had been told, and from the way Nicole remained silent, she was still working through it herself.

Within ten minutes, they were airborne again.

"Where are we going?" Michael asked.

The nearest crewmember tapped his headset then leaned over and pressed a button on the one Michael wore.

"Where *are* we going?" Michael asked again.

"We have coordinates," the crewmember replied. Like the others, he was American too, his accent as Californian as his tan.

Michael stared at him, waiting for more information. The crewmember returned his stare.

"To where, your mom's house?" Michael asked.

"I suggest you get some sleep, Doctor. It's going to be a long flight."

"It can't be as long as the last one," Nicole said, having activated her own headset microphone.

"Where did you come from?" The female pilot cut into the frequency.

"Doctor Armitage's mom's house," Nicole said with no trace of humor.

The crewmember across from Michael switched channels and said something that made the co-pilot laugh.

Conversation stopped after that, and the only sound was the teeth rattling vibration of the rotor.

Michael hadn't seen his watch or cellphone since they were picked up in Honolulu. The blackout drinking session had been on Saturday night; by his best guess, it was now Monday morning.

Except, he almost slapped his head, New Zealand was on the

other side of the International Date Line. Which meant, it was what? Tuesday… or Sunday?

The city of Auckland and the islands of New Zealand had vanished in the cloudy haze. Michael could make out the green of the South Pacific far below them. The sea was rough, each wave tipped with white foam caps. From this height, they put Michael in mind of rows of shark's teeth. There were no islands that a helicopter could reach, which meant they had to be heading to a ship. A lot of ships had helicopter-landing pads. If it was as rough down there as it looked, they might have to be winched on board.

Looking out the window, he scanned the horizon for the outline of a ship. Nothing but storm swell and the twisting shades of green ocean in all directions.

In spite of it all, Michael closed his eyes and tried to think of anything other than how the hell he was going to get out of this alive.

CHAPTER 4

"Hey, Hicks, wake up."

Michael snorted and jerked awake. "What?"

"Another day in the Marine Corp," the crewmember opposite intoned.

Michael blinked in confusion.

"Not a movie fan?"

"I–sure. Alien, right?"

"*Aliens*," Nicole corrected, glancing away from the window.

"That's what I said."

"Sure…" Nicole went back to the window.

"Suit up," the pilot ordered.

"Put this on." The crewmember worked with quick efficiency to lock Michael and then Nicole into a harness that pulled tight around the chest, shoulders, and between the legs.

"You are going to be winched to your destination. The suits you are wearing are designed to keep you alive in open water for up to an hour. If you end up in the water, pull this tab here. A life vest will inflate and you will be on the surface in seconds."

"You'll come down and pick us up though, right?" Nicole seemed to be giving the latest briefing her full attention.

"Absolutely. We will not be leaving until you are confirmed aboard."

"Aboard what?" Michael looked out at the open ocean again; no ships in sight.

A black shape, larger than a whale, broke the surface like a leviathan summoned from the primordial depths. They stared in stunned silence as the sleek cylinder shed foaming water and sliced through the dancing swell.

"Is that a submarine?" Nicole looked around, her mouth open in shock.

"No, ma'am." The crew in the cabin with them didn't even look out the window.

"A nuclear submarine? It has to be; there is no way that is a research vessel."

"Ma'am, there are no US naval vessels currently operating within New Zealand territorial waters."

"It's right there!" Nicole tapped the thick Perspex window.

"This is one of those things Mister Suit said we can never talk about," Michael said.

Nicole subsided. The calm and matter of fact nature of the lecture about what would happen if they were to reveal any information they were made privy to had scared her deeply.

The helicopter crew moved around the cramped cabin, clipping the two civilian passengers into harnesses and checking everything was secure.

"You are going to be winched out of the helo," the crewmember clipping lines to their harnesses announced. "You don't need to do anything except keep your legs together and your arms folded across your chest." He demonstrated by posing with this arms in an X pattern, hands to his shoulders.

Michael nodded and the side door of the helicopter slid open, exposing them to the roar of the rotors and the cold air of the open ocean.

"Just step out, like you are getting out of a car!" the crewmember shouted in Michael's ear.

He nodded, and felt the straps take his weight as he slipped out into the open air.

CHAPTER 5

The winch played out its wire cable as Michael looked upwards into the intent face of the crewmember guiding him down.

A moment later, something banged loudly in the rotor mast and a cloud of dense black smoke poured out in all directions. The helicopter jerked like a whipped horse and the tail boom turned as the fuselage spewed smoke.

The helicopter began to fall, accelerating Michael's descent. He tried to scream and then hit the water. It felt like being slammed into a concrete wall. The world exploded in a storm of bubbles, which became a tempest as something huge hit the water a few meters away. Michael fumbled for the tab on his suit. It floated up past his eyes and he grabbed at it as an immense weight dragged him down. Pulling the tab, he felt his suit go tight as it swelled with pressurized air.

The line on the harness strained as tight as an anchor, dragging him down into darkness. Michael struggled with it, pulling against the impossible weight taking him down.

*

On the helicopter, Nicole was given the same final briefing. "How are we getting home?" she yelled.

"What?" the crewmember shouted back.

"After this, will you come and pick us up?"

"I have no idea." The crewmember grinned. "Go on now!"

Nicole wanted to protest, to ask more questions, to be sure she wasn't being abandoned in the middle of the ocean. The helicopter shuddered and filled with a thick cloud of black smoke. Alarms wailed and the crew leapt into action, doing what they had trained for in situations just like this.

Nicole hung on to the door as the flight deck of the chopper tilted by 45 degrees. The grey sky and the green sea spun in a sickening kaleidoscope.

One of the crew crawled up to Nicole. "Get out of here!" he bellowed, the comms system having gone dead as fire spread through the electrical system.

Nicole pulled herself closer to the door, struggling to get her footing. Another loud bang; this one sounded closer and came with a scream. The other flight deck crewmember had drawn a pistol and calmly shot the pilot through her helmet, sending a spray of blood and bone onto the windshield.

He fired again, killing the co-pilot. The chopper dropped out of the sky as it tilted beyond the limit of the rotor's aerodynamics.

The gunman aimed at Nicole. She stared at him, frozen with shock. "Please..." she whispered. The air was knocked out of her in a scream as the helicopter crashed into the churning sea.

Water flooded into the chopper, sending everything swirling and crashing in a maelstrom of dark shadows.

The water turned dark as they sank. Nicole pulled herself up into an air pocket and snatched a deep breath. The gunman surfaced next to her, sending Nicole scrambling away from him in terror. Desperately searching for something to defend herself with, her hand closed around the handle of a knife. With a yell, she slashed at the gunman. He jerked back and then started flailing. Somewhere underwater, he was snagged on unseen debris and his focus went from killing Nicole to saving himself as the rising water threatened to sweep over his head.

Nicole slashed at him with the knife. She opened a gash on his cheek and he snarled, teeth bared like an enraged animal. Nicole stabbed downwards, puncturing the man's inflated suit and sending water and blood spraying into the air.

Sobbing in terror, Nicole stabbed again. The gunman's eyes went wide and unblinking and he slowly sank, leaving a swirling pool of blood to mark the spot. Nicole inhaled the last of the air and tore at the tab on her survival suit. With a *whoosh!* it inflated and she went tumbling out of the helicopter. She uncurled and got her bearing. Rising quickly, she focused on an orange shape struggling in the grasp of the winch harness.

Michael was still alive. Grabbing him, she sawed at the straps of the nylon harness with the knife. Years of surfing had trained her to hold her breath in turbulent waters for up to two minutes. She was reaching the limit of her capacity when the harness fell away and the two of them surged upwards.

*

From below, an orange blur emerged from the gloom. Nicole was rising fast, a torrent of bubbles streaming from her mouth. She aimed for Michael, as straight as an arrow and coming just as fast.

With the last seconds of air in his lungs, Michael grunted at the force of the impact. Nicole wrapped her arms and legs around him, the knife in one hand gleaming dull silver. She cut through the webbing of his harness. Black spots swelled and burst in his eyes. He struggled against the panic of certain death. The final cut was made to the harness and they burst onto the surface with a wild gasp for air.

Michael's chest heaved as he caught a splash of salt water and coughed until he almost fainted. Nicole dragged him onto his back, keeping his head above water and them both floating in the inflated embrace of their survival suits.

Men in dark survival suits and thick life vests splashed into the water around them. Someone grabbed Michael by the shoulders and legs. In less than a minute, he was lifted out of the water and laid on the pitching deck of the submarine.

"Get him below," an African American sailor with a New York accent gave orders. Michael was half-lifted and guided towards the conn tower. Once they reached the recessed ladder, the men stood behind him, letting Michael find his feet for the climb.

Nicole focused on breathing between the waves crashing over her head. Panic was tightly leashed like a savage dog that, if it broke free, would tear her composure to pieces.

They have done this a thousand times, she reminded herself. Though, exactly why the crew of a US Navy nuclear submarine would have reason to complete thousands of covert missions in the southern most parts of the Pacific was something she couldn't fathom.

She looked up into the faces of American sailors, arms outstretched, ready to seize her and bring her in safely to the black steel deck. She raised her hands and gripped their waiting arms.

"Welcome aboard, ma'am." The same officer guided her along the path towards the conning tower.

With a practiced efficiency, Nicole was taken inside the ship. The deck crew came inside, sealing the hatches behind them, and relaying confirmation to the control room that the cargo was secure. Nicole and Michael exchanged relieved looks; they were alive, for now at least.

"This way," the crewmember guiding them through the submarine said. They walked down a narrow corridor and into a control room lit by glowing consoles as complex as a space shuttle.

"Make depth twelve-hundred feet," a man who seemed to be in charge ordered.

Michael hesitated, waiting for some kind of acknowledgement, or warning speech. Finally, he cleared his throat, his voice still rough from the salt water he had swallowed. "Thanks for picking us up; hitchhiking is a real drag around here."

The man didn't move; his back remained ramrod straight and he showed no sign of even hearing Michael's attempt at ice-breaking humor.

"Mister Watts, do we have any civilians currently on board this vessel?"

"No, sir!" the crewmember standing left and slightly forward of Michael and Nicole snapped to attention.

"Is this vessel currently in the territorial waters of a friendly, sovereign nation?"

"No, sir!" Watts could have been on a parade ground. His gaze never flickered from the officer's face.

"Carry on, Mister Watts."

"Aye, sir." Watts indicated that Michael and Nicole should walk through the control room and exit via a forward hatch.

Once they were in the narrow corridor beyond, Michael spoke up. "What the hell was that about?"

"Sir?"

"I get it, we aren't officially here. But, that was bullshit."

"You aren't even here unofficially, sir."

"Christ," Nicole muttered. "If we get hurt, in trouble, or otherwise screwed? What then?"

"Best you don't find out, ma'am." Watts continued down the corridor. "You'll be assessed by medical, then I'll show you to your bunks. Please stay in them until I come back to get you."

The med-bay was a small room packed with state of the art medical equipment. Michael and Nicole were both examined quickly and thoroughly before being told they were fine; drink plenty of fluids and stay warm. The medic left them to finish dressing in the dry clothes provided.

Nicole waited until they were alone and then rounded on Michael. "The chopper was shot down!" she said in an angry whisper.

"What? By who?"

"One of the flight crew. He shot the others, and I guess he had a bomb or something to make us crash."

"That's crazy." Michael blew salt water out of his nose.

"They don't want anyone to know where we are going. They are going to write us off as dead."

Before Michael could reply, Watts appeared in the narrow doorway. "Follow me."

Michael and Nicole followed Watts into their cabin, and they squeezed into the small bunk spaces.

"What the fuck is going on?" Nicole said after a moment.

In the bunk below, Michael managed a small smile. "I have no idea. The best part is that even if we could tell anyone about it, they wouldn't believe us."

"Do you think they will have us killed, once we are no longer needed I mean?"

"The US government doesn't kill people like that."

"You have got to be kidding, right?"

"I'm sure we will be fine. We will go to some secret underwater base, where the science crew hasn't seen another human being in months, we'll get a tour of the facilities and get flown home. Simple."

"I hope you are right."

In his narrow bunk, Michael hoped he was too.

CHAPTER 6

Michael woke up with a dry mouth and a strange sense of claustrophobia. He pulled the privacy curtain on his bunk aside and looked up and down the narrow cabin. A shift change was underway, with crewmembers departing in an orderly fashion and the still-warm bunks being taken by men coming off shift.

"Rise and shine," Watts said, appearing through the hatch.

"I'm up." Nicole dropped to the floor from the higher bunk. She was fully dressed and looked fresh, making Michael wonder if she had already been to the facilities.

"Where's the bathroom?" Michael climbed out into the crowded cabin.

"End of the hall. Instructions are on the back of the door."

"Thanks." Michael worked his way through the foot traffic and took a leak. Returning to his bunk, he pulled on his jacket. Someone else was already asleep in the space.

Watts stood in the corridor with Nicole and both looked impatient to get moving.

"All set!" Michael grinned.

"Follow me." Watts marched away.

The crew worked at a hatch on the outer hull. Muffled clanks and hissing vibrated through the steel. A green light went on and Watts spun the locking wheel open, exposing a pipe dripping with salt water large enough to walk through. At the other end a second hatch stood closed. From this side, they could see the traces of barnacles and rock that worked to camouflage the surface from anyone who didn't know the exact position to look for it.

"Make a hole! Coming through!"

Watts moved the civilians aside as a pair of men in coveralls ducked into the tunnel carrying a heavy canvas satchel. From the sound of it, they used a pneumatic tool to open the locks at the far end.

"Why haven't they opened the hatch from the inside?" Nicole asked.

"Ma'am, it is better if you don't ask any questions at this time," Watts replied.

Michael shot her a quick smile and a nod. It was a good question and that the US Navy was having to break into their own facility, made him even more uneasy.

The technicians crawled out of the tunnel. "All yours," the lead technician said to Watts.

"In you go." Watts gestured towards the tunnel.

"In there?" Nicole leaned down and peered into the dripping tube.

"Pull the hatch, step through. There will be someone there waiting to meet you on the other side."

"Down the rabbit hole," Michael said with forced bravado. He climbed into the tunnel and inhaled the strong scent of salt water and hot metal. The hatch ahead of him showed signs of long exposure to the open ocean. Algae and limpets encrusted the surface, and the buildup had cracked where the locking bolts had been loosened. Michael seized the spoked wheel in the center and turned it, feeling the hydraulics deep in the mechanism take the strain, until after a dozen revolutions, the hatch swung outwards into the narrow tunnel.

Michael passed through the hatch. Beyond was a smooth, concrete-lined cylinder at least twenty feet long. Every five feet a pressure door had slid open, leaving a deep channel in the concrete structure. They advanced through the tunnel, emerging onto a steel deck at the end of a large room. Three metal stairs lead down to a concrete floor.

"Hello?" Michael called into the darkness. "Hey, can I get a light up here?"

Nicole climbed into the tunnel, doubled over and carrying two long-barrel flashlights. She handed one to Michael, like they were exchanging the baton in a relay race. He clicked it on and shone the beam into the space beyond the hatch.

"There's no one here. Hey, Watts, there's no one here."

A line of seven marines, each armed and wearing full NBC suits with gasmasks, came out of the submarine and quickly stepped into the first chamber.

"I love what you've done with the place," Michael said, looking around.

"Shut the fuck up," one of the marines growled.

The hatch in the side of the submarine swung closed, the opening vanishing as it sealed.

"Hey!" Nicole shouted. She hurried back to the outside of the black metal hull and rapped on it with her knuckles.

"Nicole." Michael turned back. "Nicole! Come on, we can go forward. They're just doing their thing, so let's do ours."

"They pushed us out like they were putting the goddamned cat out for the night," Nicole replied.

"So, let's go do cat things."

"Get your asses out here, Squints. *Move*," a marine ordered them back into the concrete room. Once Nicole climbed out of the connecting tunnel, he pushed the civilians aside and swung the hatch closed, spinning the locking wheel until it sealed tight.

The beams of their flashlights played across the walls and containers that were stacked on the floor. Everything looked industrial, steel drums, plastic-wrapped boxes, and plastic pallets stacked with unbranded food supplies.

A Marine spoke into a radio set, "Ishmael, Ishmael, this is Fire Team Beta. Sergeant Nolan confirming we are high and dry. Habitat hatch zero-delta-three is secured." He paused for a few seconds. "Sarge? Comms aren't penetrating the walls here. We're out of contact."

"Roger that, Menowski," Sergeant Nolan replied. "Troye, watch the squints. Rest of you, move out."

"Why don't we get gasmasks and hazmat suits?" Nicole asked. "Is there a biohazard here we haven't been told about?"

"Standard issue for military personnel on a mission like this," Nolan said, without giving her more than a glance.

"Military personnel only? Does that mean civilians are expendable?" Michael asked.

The marines moved without comment, M16 rifles raised and ready to fire as they slipped through the dark surroundings. The narrow beams from their lights cut through the gloom like lightsabers.

"Stay close and stay silent," the marine assigned to guard the scientists said.

Michael and Nicole meekly followed him through the room, noting the strong smell of salt water and near silence, broken only by the whir of the air-conditioning.

At the door, the fire team regrouped while Nolan keyed a code into a number pad and disengaged the locks. When the door opened, the light in the corridor glowed then flickered, sputtering and shorting out before going dark.

From the rear, Michael and Nicole could see on the opposite wall of the corridor, long scratches and dark smears of strange graffiti. The marines moved into the corridor, taking up positions facing in both directions. The hallway was bathed in flickering light and the staccato sparking of short-circuiting wires. The musty stink of piss, shit, and spilt blood mingled with the salt-water odors.

"Body, twenty feet forward. Facedown, no movement," one of the marines reported.

"Lewis, cover Nato," the sergeant ordered and the marines moved to check the body. A moment later, Nato confirmed that the body was dead.

Nicole stood next to Michael, her arms folded and a grim expression in her face.

"I'm sure it will be fine," Michael said quietly.

"Does any of this look fine to you?"

Michael shrugged.

"Sarge," Vince 'Nato' Natalo called Sergeant Nolan forward. "This guy's been dead a couple of days at least."

The sergeant crouched down and frisked the corpse for identification. The dead man had a swipe card with a blue stripe hanging from a lanyard around his neck. "Maintenance Engineer,

James Dodds," Nolan announced. "SUD has a crew of one-thirty-six. Minus one."

The civilians watched from a safe distance as the marines checked the body. "Something is wrong here," Nicole murmured.

"Yes, which is why we are here," Michael replied.

"No." Nicole looked at him, her expression grim. "That is why the marines were sent in."

"Sure, and they are going to protect us while we do the thinking."

"I hope it is that simple."

Michael shrugged. "Keep your voice down, until we find someone in charge."

"What, then we can start yelling?"

Michael was silent as they looked up and down the corridor. A number stenciled in black paint on the opposite wall said, *D8*.

"Sarge, we've got movement." The marines took positions along the walls of the corridor. Michael listened hard, hearing the slap of bare feet on the concrete. A low growling sound, wet and bronchial, drifted down the corridor.

No one moved when the first of the approaching figures emerged from the darkness at the far end of the corridor. To Michael, it looked like a regular person, hunched over, their arms hanging loosely. Their shoes were gone, and their feet were encrusted with dried blood and filth.

"Identify yourself!" Nolan barked. The approaching figure jerked his head up, sniffing the air and staring hard. "Identify yourself!" Nolan shouted again. The approaching man kept coming, picking up speed, breaking into a shuffling run, the phlegmy growl rattling deep in his chest.

"Stop!" Nolan shouted. "Stop or we will fire!"

The marines trained their rifles on the approaching man. More people appeared around the corner behind him. All of them were bloodstained and moving with stiff, jerking movements of uncoordinated limbs until they sensed the charging man ahead of them. Then they lurched forward, charging after the lead figure and filling the corridor with their snarls.

"Put them down," Nolan ordered.

The marines opened fire with calm efficiency. Each round hit its target, punching holes in the chests of the first of the oncoming pack.

The bullet wounds didn't slow them down. The soldiers adjusted their aim and a few well-placed headshots sent the front line crashing to the ground.

"Prepare for close-combat!" Nolan announced.

The marines at the front fixed their bayonets while those behind kept firing. The squad moved back in a practiced pattern as the oncoming horde reached them. The floor became slick with blood and spilled guts. Brain tissue glistened on the floor.

As the snarling crowd pressed forward, the marines engaged them with bayonets and rifle butts, knocking the enemy down and finishing them with a single shot to the head.

"Stay down!" Michael and Nicole's escort yelled. They crouched, hands pressed over their ears against the noise of the gun battle.

Nicole leaned against a door, the only shelter in the corridor. "Shit!" she yelped as the door popped open, swinging inwards and dumping her on the floor.

"Hello? Come in. How can I help you?" a female voice asked.

Nicole clambered to her feet as Michael tumbled into the room and pushed the door shut.

"Stay down!" he yelled. Something thudded against the door and they heard one of the marines shouting a warning to his comrades.

Nicole stared at an office room lit by a desk lamp. A woman wearing a lab coat over a polar fleece sweater sat at a crowded desk.

"We, well… Uhm…" Michael struggled to speak.

"Is this a drill?" she asked.

"What? No. I mean…"

"Is there another way out of here?" Nicole stood and walked closer to the desk.

"There is, but the door is locked. Perhaps you could explain why you have come crashing into my office?"

"Who the fuck are you?" Michael asked.

"Hayley Cross, Facility Logistics Manager," the woman replied.

"Pleased to meet you, Ms. Cross," Nicole said with a nod. "Could you hurry up and unlock the door?"

"Please, call me Hayley. When did you two arrive?"

Michael shot a glance at the door they had come through, the gun fire reducing to an occasional report. "Actually, we just got in. This place is certainly…different from what we had been told to expect."

Cross smiled warmly. "You get used to it. Of course, no one back on the mainland would ever believe you, even if you were allowed to speak of this place and the work being done here."

"Yeah," Nicole said. "The need for secrecy was made

perfectly clear to us."

"Hayley Cross, I don't believe we have met?" Cross said suddenly.

"I'm Doctor Michael Armitage, hydrozoan specialist," Michael said. "This is Doctor Nicole Saint-Clair, she does evolutionary genetics."

Cross nodded. "Doctor Saint-Clair, I did enjoy your paper on the transition of genes from essential to superfluous."

"Thanks," Nicole replied. "The place is… messed up."

"Is it?" Cross didn't seem phased by the muffled noises of fighting out in the corridor.

"Are you saying it was always like this?" Michael indicated a spatter of dried blood.

"I honestly haven't noticed. You must be here for Bernard. That's Doctor Saul. He's our head of research operations. Not my area of expertise at all, I'm afraid."

"Yes, that is exactly who we were hoping to meet with. Any idea where he might be?" Michael ignored Nicole's *WTF?* expression.

"I'm sure he is around here somewhere." The way Cross spoke had a saccharine cheer to it that raised the hairs on the back of Michael's neck.

"Is everything okay?" Nicole asked.

Cross jerked her head to stare at Nicole. "Of course. Everything is fine."

"It's just, well, there's quite a mess out in the corridor. It seems like there had been an accident?"

"Everything is fine. If there were any issues with this facility, I would know about it. I am the facility's logistics manager."

"Yes, you mentioned that," Michael replied.

"Wait, we were attacked. There are marines with us, soldiers. They are shooting the people who attacked us!" Nicole shouted.

"Of course. Now let me see if I can find Bernard for you."

Michael and Nicole stared in astonishment as Cross looked around her desk, as if Bernard was a lost pen or stapler.

"Does Doctor Saul have an office? Perhaps he is waiting for us there?" Michael asked.

"Yes," Cross said after a moment.

"We had best go there and find him." Michael went to the door; Nicole followed.

Cross remained at her desk for a few seconds then stood up and walked across the room. "It will be good to talk to Bernard. He has been rather uncommunicative lately."

The door behind them burst open and the marine squad charged into the room.

"Down! Everyone down!"

Michael and Nicole dropped, putting their hands over their heads as they lay down on the floor.

"What is going on here?" Cross stood behind her desk.

"Identify yourself!"

"Hayley Cross, Facilities Logistics Manager. What do you mean, barging into my office?"

"Check her ID," Nolan ordered.

Nato stepped up and yanked the ID card from around Cross' neck. "ID checks out."

"Bring her with us," Nolan commanded.

"You sure that's a good idea, Sarge? Humping three squints?" Rifleman Lewis asked.

"Are you questioning my orders, Lewis?"

"No, Sarge."

"I didn't think so. As you were, marine."

CHAPTER 7

Brubaker, the squad medic, made his report to Nolan. "She's in shock. Disorientated, cognitive problems. Physically, her vital signs are subdued, but stable."

Nolan nodded. "You get anything out of her about what happened here? Where everyone else is?"

"No, Sarge. She's fucked up."

"Okay, keep her under observation."

"Sarge?"

"Yeah, Brew?"

"What the fuck is wrong with the squints we lit up outside?"

"You're the medic, you tell me."

"I honestly don't know, Sarge."

"Exactly. We keep on mission until we have determined what the fuck is going on here and secured this facility."

"Aye, Sergeant."

Nolan stepped away. "We ready to move?"

The squad replied in the affirmative.

"Nato, on point. Rest of you, keep your eyes open."

Cross had remained silent since they took her ID. Now she cocked her head to one side in a bird-like way, as if listening to something no one else could hear.

"Where's that door go, Sarge?" Troye asked.

"Secondary corridor, through C-section."

"We gonna check it out?"

"Be my guest, Troye."

Troye tried the handle and confirmed the door was locked. "Breaching," he announced. With a well-placed kick, the door splintered and popped open.

Troye pushed the door open with one boot, his weapon sweeping the arc of the corridor on the other side. "Clear," he announced. The door wrenched wide and the space filled with snarling faces and reaching arms.

Troye jerked back and opened fire, shattering the skull of the nearest drooling face in a single shot.

"Step back, Troye!" Nolan ordered.

The marine ducked and slipped aside. With their line of fire clear, Nolan, Riflemen Caulfield, Lewis, and Menowski opened up. The loud chatter of semi-automatic weapons fire drowned out the snarling of the creatures pushing through the doorway.

Several rounds ricocheted, sending Michael and Nicole flat on the floor again.

"I am not staying here!" Nicole hissed. Michael nodded and glanced towards Troye. He was down on one knee, reloading with a practiced ease.

Michael sprang to his feet and ran for the door that opened into the D-section corridor. He threw it open, ignoring Troye's shout. Nicole launched herself after Michael, skidding in the blood and almost falling as she went through the door. Another pack of bloodstained creatures was running towards them. Down the hallway. Michael was backing away and yelling, trying to draw their attention away from Nicole.

A jet of fire erupted from behind the pack, engulfing them in the sudden inferno. Black smoke filled the corridor. Nicole collided with Michael, sending them both staggering against the wall as they tried not to choke in the spreading cloud of smoke. A moment later, a shrieking figure blundered out of the flames, careened off the wall, and toppled over.

The blast of fire cut off. "You two! Follow me!" a man's voice yelled from the swirling smoke. A digital alarm sounded at the same moment, and the sprinkler system started to flood the hallway with a dousing spray.

Nicole leapt over a blazing corpse, Michael on her heels. "What the fuck was that?" she managed.

"I have no fucking idea," he replied and they ran.

CHAPTER 8

A bearded man in a gasmask, carrying a homemade flamethrower, waved them through an open door. After Michael and Nicole ran into the room, he slammed the door, cutting off the smoke and noise of the alarm system.

The room was dry, and the bearded man gestured for them to follow him past shelves loaded with boxes of medical equipment. The hissing flamethrower he carried sputtered and went out.

"Who are you?" Michael demanded.

"Shut up and keep moving," the man replied, his voice muffled behind the gasmask. He opened a door on the other side of the room, checked the space beyond it, and then waved them through.

With no other choice but to follow, Michael and Nicole found themselves in a deserted corridor. A Chinese woman with a spiked club stepped up behind them, her weapon raised and ready to hit a home run.

"Whoa! Easy, Sue! Easy!" The bearded man waved his flamethrower until she relaxed.

"Who the fuck are they?" Sue demanded.

"We just got here!" Michael screamed.

The man looked around. "It's not safe out here. Come on."

"We're with the marines!" Michael said. "We should go back

and help them!"

He was ignored as the bearded man opened another door and pushed them through. Michael and Nicole found themselves in a dark room. Once the four of them were inside, Sue barred the door with a length of metal pipe wedged against the handle.

The bearded man pulled his gasmask off, sweat streaming down his face, leaving pale tracks on his brown skin.

"What the fuck is going on?" Michael demanded.

"I told you they weren't marines, Bernie," Sue scowled.

"Just shut up," Bernie replied. "Start with your names."

"Michael Armitage."

"Nicole Saint-Clair."

"Doctor Michael Armitage?" Sue blinked.

"Yeah?"

"Your research on hydrozoans is fascinating. I'm surprised they didn't send you here sooner."

"Thanks. Though, I don't tend to get a lot of work from the US Navy."

"Marriage was too much work for you." This came from somewhere else in the room. Michael swept the room with his flashlight. Propped up on a makeshift cot with a stained bandage wrapped around her abdomen was a woman wearing Navy fatigues, with short, dark hair and an intense stare.

"Gretchen?" Michael stared back at her.

"Hello, Mike," she replied. "If they sent you here to rescue us, then things are much worse than we thought."

"What the hell happened?" Michael went to the cot side and crouched down.

"Not sure myself…" Gretchen's face was pale and breathing

seemed to cause her pain.

"Can someone try and explain?" Nicole asked.

"Bernie?" Sue asked.

Now that the moments of adrenaline-filled action had passed, the bearded man looked like he might be about to collapse himself. "I'm not entirely sure either..."

"Just tell us what you know," Nicole said.

"Something has happened to the crew of this installation," Bernie said. "We don't know exactly what, but it seems permanent and they are..." he trailed off.

"They are no longer human," Sue stated. "They are not human and they are dangerous."

"Was that woman, Hayley Cross, one of them?" Michael asked.

Bernie started to shake his head. "I think so? I mean... it's complicated."

"We saw the video. That was you, right? Bernard Saul?" Nicole asked.

"Yeah. Someone took it seriously. We had a squad of marines here within twenty-four hours."

"You had marines in here before we arrived?" Michael asked.

"Great," Nicole breathed with relief. "Where are they?"

"Dead or infected," Sue replied.

"Listen," Nicole insisted. "We are with a squad of marines. These guys are serious, professional soldiers. They took out a lot of the – the people that attacked us."

"The first squad of marines was professional too," Gretchen said. "Real ass-kickers. Experienced. Highly trained and, ultimately, casualties."

"Cross seemed human enough," Nicole said. "I mean, she was a little weird, but she was definitely human."

"They look human. Right up to the point where they don't," Bernie said.

"Is everyone else… what, dead?" Michael asked.

"I think so," Sue replied. "Kincaid and a couple of marines were holed up in the water reclamation station, but we haven't heard from them since yesterday."

"They might be okay," Bernie spoke up.

"They might be dead!" Sue snarled.

"Okay, okay." Michael waved for silence. "There's a US Navy submarine docked with this facility. We need to get back there and get them to do whatever it is that they do in situations like this."

"Situations like this? Chri–" Gretchen broke off in a convulsive cough. "*Shit…*" she muttered. Michael lifted a towel and dabbed the blood from her lips.

"We need to get you to the sub. You need medical attention," Michael said.

"Yeah, I'm not going anywhere. If we bring more marines or anyone else in here, they're going to end up as dead as we are."

"We're not dead yet," Michael said.

Gretchen moved her gaze to stare at him, "I'm sorry to see you. I mean, in this place."

"I didn't know you were here," Michael admitted.

"Of course you didn't. Even if we were still talking, I couldn't have told you anything about my assignment."

"Well, I'm here now. Care to explain what this place is?"

"No harm in telling you now I guess," Bernard spoke up.

"During the Cold War, billions of dollars were spent in developing underwater submarine bases at strategic points around the world. This was one of the last commissioned, and by the 1980s, defense ideas had changed. Most of the bases were either flooded or demolished. I have heard that there are three left, including this one. Only one of the others is still being used for surveillance of submarine traffic. The other one has been turned over to research, like this place."

"What kind of research?" Nicole had asked the same question of Mr. Suit and she still wanted a clear answer.

"All kinds," Sue replied. "Virology, genetics, chemical warfare, alien environment survival. We had a guy here for six months who was trying to train cockroaches to be astronauts."

"Animals are being sent into space all the time," Michael said. "I'm pretty sure cockroaches have logged more hours in orbit than people."

"That may be true," Sue replied. "But this guy was training them to fly tiny rockets and manipulate complex machines. He wanted to send these trained roaches to Mars and have them pilot a roach-sized craft there, land it, conduct experiments and then, return."

"Did it work?" Michael asked, intrigued in spite of his cynicism.

"I don't know. What I can tell you is that after six months, he had cockroaches doing things that no roach should be able to do. Then he left, took his equipment with him, and we never heard anything more about it."

"If it had worked, we would have heard about it," Nicole spoke up.

Sue regarded her steadily. "Like you knew everything about the SUDS before you signed up for this?"

"Well no, but…"

"What does SUD stand for?" Michael asked.

"Submarine Underground Defense Structure. You're standing in SUD-8," Bernard explained.

"Great," Nicole straightened, "can we leave now?"

Michael nodded. "I agree, back to the sub. Get the fuck out of here."

Bernard sighed and hefted the launch tube of his flamethrower. "We can't let anyone leave."

"Why the hell not?" Nicole demanded.

"Until we know exactly what the vector of infection is, we have to all stay sealed in here."

"That's bullshit," Nicole snapped. "Clearly we are not infected!"

"Okay! Hey! Everyone calm down!" Michael walked between Nicole and Bernard. "Doctor Saul, Bernard? You've been in touch with the Navy, right? They know what the situation is?"

Bernard nodded. "Yes. When the marines arrived, the Death Valley Protocol was cancelled. They had an override code and things were still pretending to be normal. That was over forty-eight hours ago. We have been in hiding since then."

"Hiding from the others?" Nicole asked.

"Yes."

"How many are there?"

Bernard sighed and cradled the flamethrower while he rubbed his eyes. "Ahh… there were about a hundred and forty of us on site. Then the marines; there were what? Twelve of them?"

Sue nodded. "Yes. Twelve marines came in."

"By yesterday," Bernard continued, "there were just the three of us."

"That we know of," Sue interrupted. "There might be others."

"Bernard, we saw the video you sent. What else can you tell us?" Nicole started pacing up and down.

"People started changing. The first was Andrew Filden, a lab technician. He was missing for a day, and he had no explanation for his absence. When Andrew came back, one of the Navy crew disappeared. When he was found, he had no answers either. Then more people started disappearing, just not being around one moment and then, within twenty-four hours, they turned up again with no explanation for their lost time. The effect spread exponentially. Two, four, eight, sixteen. By the time I saw the pattern, it was too late."

"Tell them about Doctor Nakiro," Sue added.

"Yes, Doctor Nakiro," Bernard continued. "She was our chief medical officer. I talked to her about doing blood tests. Then she disappeared. When she came back, she insisted everything was fine."

Sue gave a derisive snort.

"Yeah, they'd gotten her too."

"Exactly what is responsible?" Michael asked.

Bernard lowered the flamethrower and set it down carefully at his feet. "We don't know."

"Something new must have entered the closed environment," Nicole said while continuing to pace. "Some new parasite, bacterium, or virus? Some kind of toxic poisoning? Bad food? Illicit drugs?"

"There was no sign of drugs and we all ate the same food," Bernard replied. "If I can get back into the lab on level three, then I can start checking the recent specimens for anything that might… do that to a person."

"What are the initial symptoms?"

"Hayley Cross; her hand was changing," Sue said. "I hardly noticed at the time. I don't know of any biological agent that could do that to human tissue, without fever, inflammation, other symptoms."

"We don't know what the first symptoms are," Bernard replied. "It's not like I've had a chance to study any of them under laboratory conditions."

"You said Cross's skin was changing. Changing how?" Michael asked.

Sue thought hard for a moment. "It was starting to glow, turning translucent, like jelly…"

"*Mesoglea,*" Michael said absently. "The translucent material between the two layers of membranous skin on your standard jellyfish. If a person had tissue like that, they would be dead."

"I've seen others. They had skin patches that were going the same way," Sue's voice dropped to a shocked whisper. "They weren't dead. Dead people don't do what they did to Xue, or Chun."

"Some don't survive," Bernard said. "Simon was our galley manager. He tore his own eyes out and ripped off most of his face. It was like he was trying to dig into his own skull. He died before whatever it is finished with him."

"How many dead, do you think?" Michael asked.

"Twenty? Thirty?" Sue replied. She and Bernard exchanged

looks and shrugged. "Honestly, we don't know. Bodies disappear."

"There's a body, a man, back in the corridor where Bernard found us. Half his head is missing, and his brain is gone."

"Did you touch him?" Sue asked.

"I guess?" Michael replied.

Bernard snatched up his flamethrower and clicked the lighter under the muzzle until the pilot flame flared blue.

"Hey! He's fine! He barely touched the body!" Nicole pushed in front of Michael.

"*Bernard!*" Gretchen's voice was rough, but she spoke with authority. "Stand down!"

Bernard's grip on the flamethrower was white-knuckled. He looked from Michael to Nicole and then at Gretchen. "You know this guy, right?"

"Yeah," Gretchen said. "You could say that."

"Gretchen is my wife," Michael said with a shrug.

"Wow…" Nicole said.

"You came here for her?" Sue glared at Michael.

"No. I had no idea Gretchen was here. We've been, what? Separated? On a break? Shit, I don't know. We haven't seen each other in about four months now."

"I shipped out here eighteen days after you didn't respond to my final text," Gretchen said.

"I didn't get your damned text. I was on a boat in the middle of the Pacific Ocean." Michael's tone suggested that this was an argument he had been waiting to have for a long time.

"You had a goddamned satellite phone. You could have totally made contact!" Gretchen sat up, one hand pressed against the stained bandage around her abdomen.

"I get back from my research trip, can't reach you, and I don't hear from you. All the fucking Navy will tell me is that you are on a deployment and can't be reached."

"Well, they weren't wrong."

"You could have said more than a fucking text! We were married, for fuck's sake. You don't end a marriage by text!"

Gretchen's eyes narrowed. "You're telling me I ended our marriage? You were off on your damned research trips nine months of the year."

Michael closed his mouth, suddenly aware that everyone was staring at them.

"This is why we can't be married," Gretchen said, the bitterness in her voice more resigned now.

"This is not the time, or the place," Michael said.

"No shit," Nicole said.

"Who are you? His girlfriend?" Gretchen started to stand, gritting her teeth and leaning on the wall for support.

Nicole looked surprised, "What? No. I'm just here on Navy business."

"You don't look Navy. You look like the kind of surfer girl Michael always trips and lands on after a few drinks."

"Hey, fuck you!"

"Michael's sloppy seconds? I don't think so."

"Seriously?" Nicole looked to Michael who managed to wince and shrug in the same gesture.

"Don't look to him for help; it never did me any good." Gretchen stood, her face pale and her lips blue.

"You should be resting." Sue left her position by the door and went to Gretchen's side.

"I've been resting. Now it's time to do something."

"What can we do?" Bernard asked.

"We can fight. Find weapons and destroy every infected person. Bring this place back under control."

Nicole shook her head. "That's crazy. We should be finding Sergeant Nolan and his men. They can contact the submarine and get more armed marines in here. They are trained to deal with this kind of thing, right?"

Gretchen let her gaze slide across the others. "Are you not listening? They sent marines in here, and they failed. The people who are still alive are in this room. I know who I would rather have with me on this mission."

"We just got here…" Nicole whispered.

"And if you want to leave again, then work with us," Sue snapped.

"Okay! Okay…" Michael took a turn pacing up and down. "What is the plan?"

"Simple," Gretchen said. "Get to the nearest laboratory. MacGyver some weapons, like Bernie's flamethrower. Then we sweep through this place. We burn everything organic. Destroy the infectious agent and its hosts. Once the place is sterile, we send confirmation to the mainland and they let us leave."

"What about the Death Valley Protocol?" Nicole said, and the others all looked at her in surprise.

"What do you know about that?" Gretchen asked.

"Enough," Nicole replied.

"It could be activated. The marines that came in, and they shut it down," Bernard said.

"I still don't understand how it works," Nicole said.

"You don't need to know," Gretchen replied.

Michael continued circling. "They are going to want to know what happened. They'll want samples, research data, and some kind of explanation."

"We can tell them," Bernard said, nodding. "Our data is backed up to off-site servers. Everything we know, they will know."

"Everything?" Nicole asked.

Bernard nodded. "Yeah."

Nicole regarded him steadily. "If that were true, they don't need you, or any of us."

Sue and Bernard looked at the floor.

Nicole gave a short humorless laugh. "You have something that the admiral or the government or whoever it is that stirs this pot of shit wants to get their hands on?"

"When things started going weird… we stopped some of the data feeds into the backup system," Bernard replied.

"To avoid raising suspicions, we kept enough data flowing. We kept some of our local data on tape. They're in a secure locker off an empty lab on this level."

Michael blinked. "That's your plan? You think you have some information that will buy you a ticket off the island?"

"We're not on an island," Gretchen replied.

"We're cut off in a remote location with no easy way of returning to the world. *We are on a fucking island*," Michael said.

"Semantics aside," Gretchen said. "We should recover that data and anything else we can find to buy our way out of here."

"I'm not sure that will be enough," Nicole said. "Someone tried to kill us on the way here."

They listened in silence as she recounted the events leading to their covert departure from Hawaii and the strange briefing with the man in the suit.

"Then the chopper was sabotaged and the crew was shot. We got rescued by a goddamned US Navy submarine," Michael explained. "There is nothing OK about any of this. The entire mission is a complete cluster-fuck. That's a military term, right?" He looked at Gretchen who closed her eyes and sighed.

"I knew it," Bernard said. "We are so very fucked. This entire thing is being black-booked. No traces, no accountability. Zero witnesses. We step out and they will shoot us down and flood the entire facility."

"There must be a way to escape?" Nicole looked up. "I mean, where are we exactly?"

Bernard snorted. "There's no way out of here, except the way you came in."

"What he means," Sue picked up the dropped thread of conversation as Bernard slumped, "is that you are currently twelve-thousand feet below the surface. We are deep in the Kermadec Trench. There is nothing down here; just us and the life forms that have been crawling around in the abyss for millions of years. We're so far away from our world, we may as well be on Mars."

"Gee, if only the cockroach astronauts were still here, I'm sure they could fly us home," Nicola said, her voice dripping with sarcasm.

"If they were here, the military might actually come back to save them. Humans are expendable. Super smart roaches? Probably not."

"I hear something." Sue tensed, her body almost quivering as she listened.

CHAPTER 9

"No sign of them, Sarge." Troye stood to attention, his eyes fixed on the wall opposite, not blinking as Sergeant Nolan glared at him from two inches away.

"Sarge isn't here right now. You are addressing Sergeant Nolan, Marine. You were ordered to protect and escort the civilian scientists, Troye."

"Yes, Sergeant."

"If they are dead, we have failed one of our mission parameters. Do you want to fail one of our mission parameters?" Nolan spoke in a cold whisper.

"No, Sergeant."

"Then get the fuck out there and find them. Bring them back to me and do not, I repeat, do-fucking-not, fuck this up."

"Yes, Sergeant."

"Brubaker, is our remaining civilian ready to move?"

"Yes, Sarge."

Cross didn't react when Brubaker spoke to her. He ended up taking her arm and standing her up. "C'mon, lady, time to go."

"Let's move." Nolan led his team out into the corridor and past the corpses that steamed under the dripping fire sprinkler system.

They opened each locked door in turn, checking each room on

level seven in a routine they had drilled a hundred times.

"This section is clear, Sarge," Troye reported.

Nolan unfolded a laminated sheet retrieved from his combat vest. "There's a corridor on the other side of this section. We're wasting time, keep moving."

"Yes, Sergeant."

With Nato on point, the squad crossed into the parallel corridor. He signaled when he heard voices, low and intense from behind a closed door.

The squad took up their positions, ready to breach and secure the room. At Nolan's go-signal, they smashed the door in with a single kick.

"Get down! Get down!" the squad filled the room, yelling instructions and shoving Bernard and Sue to the floor.

Michael hesitated for a moment and then went to the floor too.

"Nolan? It's us! Armitage and Saint-Clair!" Nicole yelled from where she was being pressed, face down, into the concrete.

"Got a wounded woman back here!" Nato yelled.

"Anything else?" Nolan replied.

"Clear!" the marine reported.

"Who are you people?" Nolan demanded.

Introductions were made quickly. Bernard and Sue's identity was verified by a quick check of the photo ID cards they carried.

"I'm Sergeant Nolan, US Marines. We have orders to secure and this facility."

"Sergeant, Lieutenant Gretchen Armitage, US Navy. I'm part of the security assignment for this facility."

"Lieutenant." Nolan snapped a salute. Gretchen returned it.

"Your ride still docked?" Gretchen asked.

"Yes, ma'am."

"We can't leave yet. This facility is experiencing a medical emergency. We are under quarantine until the source of the infectious agent is confirmed and isolated."

"My orders are different, Lieutenant."

"And what are your orders, Sergeant?"

"Secure the facility. Prevent any compromised personnel from leaving. Obtain a sample of whatever is causing the infection and return with it to the boat."

"Sounds reasonable. You have any clue what is going on?"

"Ma'am, so far my men and I have encountered people suffering some kind of psychotic rabies, and a woman who is in deep shock."

"It's not rabies," Bernard said.

"Excuse me?" Nolan turned on him.

"It's not rabies. Rabies presents in an entirely different way. There's no fever with this condition, no photophobia, no hydrophobia."

"Goddamned place is full of squints," Troye muttered.

Nolan pondered for a moment. "All right, Brubaker, check the lieutenant's wound. Put the civilians in here, we complete our sweep and pick them up on the way out."

"Aye, Sarge."

The squad made ready to move out. Cross was put in a corner, where she sat, smiling blankly and staring at nothing.

Nolan checked the hallway. "Brubaker, Caulfield, stay here and provide security to the civilians and the lieutenant. Rest of you, with me."

In the silence left after the squad's departure, Michael could hear his own breath. He wondered how long he had been holding it.

"How long are they going to be?" Nicole asked.

Gretchen waved a hand. "There's seven levels to this facility. We are in level seven, the basement. The top two are facilities plant. Water reclamation, power generation, air-conditioning. Not a lot of space to move around. That means they have four levels to search for survivors and the infected. They'll be away for a few hours at least. I suggest you get some sleep."

Nicole shivered. Right now she was sure she would never sleep again.

.

CHAPTER 10

A woman's body lay twisted on the landing, her neck broken and a dried pool of bodily fluids crusted around her.

"She one of ours?" Nolan asked.

Menowski straightened up. "Negative, ID says she's Leanne Carbello."

"Keep moving; watch for Tangoes."

Menowski stepped over the corpse and moved up the stairs, his M16 raised and sweeping the concrete stairs ahead. At the next landing, he moved to cover the stairs that went up while the rest of the squad took their positions.

A solid steel door with a round window of thick glass and a locking wheel in the center of it blocked access to the floor off the stairwell.

"Level six, Sarge," Menowski spoke into his radio.

"Check. Open it up and let's take a look."

Nato and Menowski covered the door while Lewis and Brubaker turned the wheel on the steel door. As it opened, water poured out around their feet

"Got some kind of leak up here, Sarge," Troye reported.

"How bad is it?"

"Few inches. Barely get your boots wet."

"Try not to drown, Troye." Nolan came up the stairs behind

his squad.

The marines went through the door, stepping each way and covering the corridor in both directions. The main lights were out on this floor; only the red emergency egress lighting in wire cages on the wall still glowed.

"Check this shit out." Nato nodded towards a line of bullet holes along a wall.

"Marines," Lewis said. "Ain't no one else got them steady hands."

"Except maybe your mom," Troye said automatically.

"Tangoes." Lewis pulled his rifle in tight and sighted down the barrel. In the shadows, dark figures rose from where they knelt on the floor.

"What are they doing? Praying to Allah or some shit?" Troye asked.

"Get down! On your knees! Put your hands behind your head!" Nato shouted at the advancing people. They kept coming, walking with their eyes open and unblinking into the beams of the marine's flashlights.

"Light 'em up," Nolan ordered.

The steady crack of weapons fire filled the air. Dull echoes rebounded off the walls and each shot was on target, dropping the advancing infected by blowing out the back of their skulls.

"Tangoes down," Lewis confirmed.

With careful steps, the marines moved down the corridor, checking each corpse as they passed.

At the next intersection, they looked both ways. More bodies lay floating in the shallow water. Nato sighted in on the nearest one and mentally dared it to move. The body took the dare and lifted his dripping head. Nato fired, the shot punching a hole in the rising figure's skull. The man dropped with a splash. Others started standing, low guttural sounds coming from a dozen throats.

"We got more behind us," Lewis warned.

"Put them down. Put them all down," Nolan ordered.

Lewis opened fire. This wasn't combat; it wasn't even range shooting. This was like shooting fish in a very shallow barrel.

The infected lumbered towards them, starting to run when whatever was left of their brains sent the message to their bodies to kill and devour the marines gunning them down.

"Watch your backs!" Menowski reminded his comrades. He took the wall opposite Lewis and matched him shot for shot.

"Reloading," Troye shouted. He reached for a new magazine and slapped it into his rifle. In that few seconds of distraction, the door beside him opened and a woman pounced with a gurgling snarl.

"Fuck!" Troye yelled. Splashing in the dark water, he punched his attacker in the face. The woman's teeth snapped at his face, biting into the gloves he wore.

Lewis aimed. "Can't get a clear shot!"

Nolan stormed past the marine and kicked the snarling woman in the head. She tumbled away and Troye scrambled to his feet. Lewis fired twice, busting the infected woman's skull with each shot.

"Shape up, Troye!" Nolan yelled.

"Yes, Sarge!"

More infected came out of the room, stumbling over each other and landing in the water. Troye opened fire, burning with embarrassment from Nolan's reprimand. The squad hammered the infected with controlled fire.

In less than a minute, the charge was broken and a pile of fresh corpses lay at their feet.

"The fuck is this shit?" Lewis asked.

"What you got?" Nolan replied.

Lewis gestured with the muzzle of his rifle at a white lump pulsing in a gaping head wound. "I seen brains before, Sarge. That ain't brains."

Nolan scowled. His briefing had been short on details, but he understood that anything strange was to be secured and returned to the mainland for further study.

"Troye, Nato, cover me." Nolan unslung the rucksack on his back and retrieved a steel cylinder with a biohazard sticker in bright yellow on the outside. Twisting it open, he retrieved a pair of steel tongs from inside and grabbed the pulsing lump. It stilled for a moment and he pulled on it. Nolan was surprised by the way it resisted, as if gripping the inside of the dead man's head.

"What the fuck is that, Sarge?" Lewis moved in for a closer look.

"I have no fucking idea," Nolan said quietly. The white jelly-like lump came away from the dead man, long translucent tendrils stretching all the way inside the cooling wound.

The threads went taut as Nolan tugged, then in an instant, they snapped, whipping around, using the momentum to rip free from the pincer grip and hit Nolan in the face.

"Fuck!" Nolan yelled. He dropped the container and dragged at the mess clinging to his face.

Troye and the others started laughing.

"Shit, Sarge! I think it likes you!"

Nolan scraped at the jelly with one hand. It slithered across his skin and the tendrils slipped around his neck. The wet blob slid up his cheek and pressed against his ear.

"Get this fucking thing off me!"

Lewis stopped laughing as Nolan's expression went from shock to sudden pain.

"Shit, Sarge?"

Nolan convulsed, his back arching and his weapon dropping with a splash as the lump pulsed on the side of his head.

"Sarge?" Lewis snatched the white jelly and yelped, shaking his gloved hand. "Fucking thing stung me right through my fucking glove!"

Nolan went rigid, his lips pulling back from his gritted teeth in a rictus grin. Froth hissed out of his mouth and he toppled backwards. The sergeant's head struck the wall with a dull thud and he slid to the floor.

Nato slapped the marine next to him on the shoulder. "Troye! Get Brubaker! Now damnit!"

Troye stared in shock at Nolan and then nodded, running down the corridor towards the stairwell.

Lewis slung his rifle and crouched to check on Nolan. "Do not touch him!" Nato yelled.

"The fuck, man? Sarge is injured!"

"Whatever the fuck that is, it came out of one of those crazy motherfuckers. You don't want to catch what they have."

"No fucking way." Lewis stood up and aimed his rifle at Nolan, who lay still in the water.

"Don't shoot him either," Nato warned. "He's still Sergeant Nolan."

"The fuck is going on here, Nato?" Lewis looked genuinely unsettled for the first time since they disembarked.

"Fuck if I know, man. But we keep our shit tight. Brubaker will fix the Sarge."

"This isn't what we do, man. Shooting sick people, getting fucked up by some weird boogers."

"What we do is follow orders." Nato glanced up and down the corridor. "We should find somewhere dry to make the sergeant comfortable."

"I don't think we should leave him," Lewis replied.

"He's not going anywhere. With me, marine." Nato moved off into the darkness, scanning the corridor with his flashlight, ready to fire on anything that came at him.

CHAPTER 11

Muffled voices, an urgent conversation, and then running feet moving away down the corridor.

"What the fuck was that?" Bernard asked.

No one rushed for the door. It fell to Michael to open it and peer outside. "The marines are gone," he reported.

Slipping out, Michael stood with his back against the corridor wall as the others silently followed.

Gretchen had drawn a heavy automatic pistol from somewhere. Michael couldn't guess the make, model, or caliber. She prepped it with a casual and professional ease.

"The level seven labs are this way," Bernard said, indicating with the hissing muzzle of the flamethrower.

"Lead the way," Gretchen said.

*

The lights flickered on in a strobe of fluorescent charge. Bernard swept the laboratory with the flamethrower, making Michael uneasy about what would happen if he squeezed the trigger and unleashed a storm of fire on the well-stocked shelves of chemicals.

"Where's the lock up?" Nicole asked.

"Through there." Sue stepped around Bernard and hurried

across the room. She stopped to key a code into a panel and twisted the handle. "Give me one–" The door exploded in a storm of snarling teeth and flailing hands.

Sue screamed as the infected poured out of the next room. A marine with a facemask of congealed blood howled and threw himself at the woman. Sue went down, beating the shit out of the man until he sank his teeth into her cheek and ripped the flesh away in a dripping chunk.

Bernard screamed and jerked on the trigger of his flamethrower. The muzzle flared and choked, a puff of flame fading to smoke.

"Shit!" he yelled and fumbled for the pump lever at the bottom of the tank. Working it frantically, he kept looking at the jam of squirming bodies in the doorway.

"I could use some fucking help here!"

Gretchen put her pistol to the head of the marine savaging Sue's corpse. She squeezed the trigger, and his body jerked in a spray of brain and bone.

The knot of struggling bodies spewed blood and snarls as Gretchen started shooting into them. Heads exploded and blood spurted as the rounds hit their targets with lethal accuracy.

"Shut the fucking door!" Bernard yelled.

Michael ran across the room, skidding in a pool of blood and crashing into a glass door cabinet on the wall. He stumbled and threw his weight against the door.

"Nicole! Help me here!"

Nicole had been standing in mute shock, staring at Sue's torn remains. She shook herself and ran to help Michael. Gretchen's gun clicked dry.

"I'm out!" she reported with a chilling calm.

Bernard triggered the flamethrower and spewed burning fuel into the doorway. Behind the door, Michael and Nicole cringed against the surge in heat. The room quickly filled with the black-smoke stench of burning flesh.

"Bernard! Ease off! Cease fire!" Gretchen had crouched low under the smoke. Nicole felt the pressure on the door ease and she slumped down, covering her face with a sleeve.

"Is the data safe?" Michael asked.

Any response was drowned out by the sudden blast of the extinguisher systems. The air filled with sodium bicarbonate powder. It rained down like a blizzard of dandruff and smothered the flames.

"Can't...breathe..." Nicole gasped. The survivors crawled out of the lab, escaping into the hallway and gulping fresh air.

"That didn't go quite as planned," Michael wheezed.

"When the smoke clears, we can try again," Gretchen replied.

"Sue is dead," Bernard whispered.

"Yes. Which means she's no longer hurting or afraid." Gretchen dropped the empty magazine out of the pistol.

"They ate her..." Bernard's voice shook.

Gretchen rounded on him. "Bernard, get your shit together. You did a good thing. You saved the rest of us. Sue's death wasn't your fault."

"I'm going back in," Michael said. He kept low, his shirt over his mouth and nose, breathing against the smoke and chemical dust. The pile of bodies in the room beyond the lab was melted together in a mosaic of blackened skin and red-raw flesh.

He pulled on the door, grimacing as the half-cooked flesh of the knot of corpses ripped, spilling steaming viscera and foul stench onto the floor. Michael gagged and held his breath; jumping over the pile was impossible. He gingerly stepped, feeling the crunch of crispy skin under foot. The room beyond the lab was stained with smoke and the smeared bodily fluids of the infected who had been trapped in there.

A filing cabinet stood in one corner, the large dial lock on the front suggesting it might contain the data tapes Sue had referred to. On the off-chance that the cabinet was unlocked, Michael tugged on the handle of the top drawer. It slid open and he jumped back in surprise.

"Christ…" he muttered. The drawer contained a small pile of papers and Manila folders. No sign of anything that could be data tapes. Taking another breath, he held it again and flicked through the folder contents. Lots of pages stamped TOP SECRET. The content of the pages was mostly blacked out. Some of them showed signs of being hastily burned and shredded.

He pulled open the second drawer: black plastic containers. Michael cracked one open, it was empty. He went through the others; all empty.

The third drawer held two ring-binder folders and a couple of technical manuals for an autoclave and an incubator.

Taking a handful of the damaged papers, Michael slipped them into his jacket and left the room. He stopped when he saw something oozing out of the steaming pile of shit that was the tangle remains of the infected.

Michael froze, hoping that it was just fluid pressure. The blackened crust of a burnt skull cracked like a hard-boiled egg. Michael wrinkled his nose at the new stench. A translucent lump pushed its way out through the spreading crack. To Michael, it looked like a birth, a hatching of something from a protective shell.

The white gel-like form pushing its way free was about the size of Michael's fist. He stared at it, thinking how it looked like a jellyfish.

It is a jellyfish... The realization came to him in a rush. It was something he could understand. In all the madness of the last few days, this was something familiar, and he found that reassuring.

"How did you get there, little guy?" he asked the white lump. The jelly lay pulsing on the steaming heap of twisted corpses. Michael looked around and took a pair of long tweezers from a laboratory tray. He gently poked at the jelly, lifting the edge of its skirt to see the hidden forms under it.

A thick tendril lashed out and wrapped around the metal tool. Michael jerked his hand back as the tweezers were yanked from his grip.

"Heh..." Michael grinned in spite of the horror of it all. Among all this, a jellyfish was still doing everything it could to survive. *Where the hell did it come from?*

"Doctor Armitage?" Bernard called from the corridor.

"Yeah?"

"Did you find the data tapes?"

Michael walked out of the lab. "I found cases, but they're empty."

"What?" Bernard shuffled the flamethrower in his arms and went to look for himself.

"Everything okay?" Nicole emerged from across the hall where she and Gretchen had been looking for weapon components.

Michael nodded. "Kinda. Let's go back in and I'll explain to you and Gretchen."

Both women listened in silence as Michael explained about the unlocked filing cabinet and the empty tape cases.

Bernard returned looking puzzled. "Lot of people had access to that filing cabinet," he said.

"Yes, but very few people knew what was being stored in there," Gretchen reminded him.

"Sue didn't know the tapes were gone. If she did, she wouldn't have opened the door," Michael said.

"Someone shoved the infected in there and closed the door to cover their tracks?" A dark expression crossed Gretchen's face. Michael recognized it from the fights that had marred the last eighteen months of their five-year marriage.

"Who the fuck would do that?" Bernard looked like he wanted to throw his hands up in the air, but the weight of the flamethrower barrel kept them still.

"Shh…" Nicole stood by the door and now waved a hand to silence the conversation. "There's someone out there…"

They listened, ears straining to hear more than the blood pounding in their ears. A wet gurgling sound came from the other side of the door. Then something slapped against it.

Gretchen waved for everyone to be still. She still gripped her pistol, even though it was empty.

Nicole's nose wrinkled; the smell of burnt flesh and boiled body fluids hung in the air, but now it was richer and even more cloying.

They stood in silence, staring at the door and waiting for another sound. Long seconds passed then the door shuddered under a heavy blow. Nicole backed away, and Bernard started pumping the pressure lever on his homemade flamethrower.

The door boomed as it was struck again. A long crack appeared in the length of the door. The reinforced wood splintered and bowed inwards.

"You ready to burn whatever comes through that door?" Gretchen asked.

Bernard nodded, flicking his cigarette lighter to set the pilot light on the flamethrower burning.

The door shattered, sending shards of wood across the room. An arm, burnt black and oozing fluid, reached through the hole. It grasped at the air and was joined by a second arm, then a third. Burnt skin hung in ragged strips from the torn flesh. The raw meat of the arm was filleted to the bone on the ragged spines of the shattered door.

"Bernard..." Gretchen warned as the scientist continued flicking his lighter.

"Fuck...fuck...fuck..." he whimpered. The door split further, the panel tearing apart under the onslaught. The thing that pushed through the gap was the scorched remains of the bodies piled up in the lab, melted together and moving chaotically with too many limbs. The mess of body parts lashed out and grabbed at Bernard. He backed away, tripping and falling on his ass.

The flamethrower spewed burning fuel as Bernard tumbled. A jet of flame arced up the wall and across the ceiling. The room filled with smoke and intense heat. Michael and the others started clubbing the monstrous knot of body parts with scraps of furniture and the remains of the door.

Gretchen grabbed a long dagger-like sliver of the door and

stabbed into the center of the writhing mess. A guttural scream came from somewhere deep in the ball of blackened flesh. Blood and yellow liquid sprayed as Gretchen's makeshift knife stabbed deep.

Nicole smashed a wooden chair over an arm that tugged at her ankle. She kept hammering at it until the bones broke and the flesh was an ochre smear on the concrete.

The blaze spread across the ceiling, dripping burning oil onto everything and setting new fires on the walls and floor.

"We have to get out of here!" Michael yelled. His eyes were streaming from the smoke and he wished the automated fire-control systems would hurry up and activate.

Gretchen howled in rage and pain, and the quivering lump in front of her finally went still. She kicked it one more time and then climbed over it and into the hallway.

"Come on!" she yelled.

Nicole ran blindly, her arms outstretched and her clothes smoldering with burning embers. Michael guided her to the doorway and helped her through. Turning back, he grabbed Bernard by the boots and dragged him to the door. The flamethrower had gone out, its reserves of fuel used up. Gasping for air, Michael stripped the flamethrower off Bernard's back and heaved the man onto his shoulder. Staggering under the extra weight, Michael crashed out of the burning room.

"Don't stop!" Gretchen shouted at him. Over the noise of the spreading fire, Michael heard the snarling growls of more infected coming after them.

CHAPTER 12

On the count of three, the marines lifted Nolan and laid him out on a cleared table in a mess room.

Brubaker continued his examination. Nolan's pulse was slow and erratic, his respiration shallow and labored. The medic carefully probed the sergeant's skull for crush injuries.

"It went inside his head, Brew," Lewis said.

"Yeah, you said that already." Brubaker could see no sign of the jelly lump that the marines insisted had crawled out of the dead man's skull and ambushed Nolan.

Nolan's ear canal showed signs of fresh bleeding, but a cursory examination showed nothing blocking it.

"He fell, right?" Brubaker asked.

"Yeah, but the fucking thing went all up in his ear first," Lewis insisted.

"I fucking heard you, Lewis." Brubaker opened Nolan's right eyelid and waved his flashlight in it. The pupil didn't contract. Then, a moment later, a line swept across his eye, like a second eyelid or windshield wiper.

Brubaker dismissed it as a trick of the light, then he saw the same dark line coil in the darkness of Nolan's pupil.

"Okay, there's definitely something in there," he agreed.

"What do we do? You can get it out, right?" Lewis looked at

Brubaker with a fearful certainty. Brubaker was a marine medic, trained and experienced in handling all kinds of traumatic injuries from gunshot wounds to burns. This shit might even puzzle a specialist in parasitology.

"The Sarge is stable. That thing inside his head hasn't killed him yet. If it's what is making the others crazy, then we have some time before Nolan wakes up and starts trying to eat us."

"We can get him fixed before then?" Lewis looked ready to shoot Nolan where he lay.

"If we can get him back to the sub, then maybe. There's a fully equipped medical team on board. They can do things we never could."

"There's gotta be medical stuff here. Like a clinic or an operating theatre?"

"Sure," Brubaker replied. "Are you a neurosurgeon, Lewis? You been holding out on us and secretly have an IQ of one-forty?"

"No," Lewis replied, sulkily.

"Well shut the fuck up and let me do what I can for the Sarge."

Lewis went to hang with Nato and the rest of the squad. Brubaker covered Nolan with a blanket and stared at the still body.

"You hungry?" Caulfield asked from the galley window.

"What's good here?" Brubaker asked.

"I wouldn't wanna eat anything I didn't hump in here myself, but they have plenty of food in cans and freeze dried. If the electricity can be trusted, the freezer back here has got sides of beef hanging in it."

"MRE it is then," Brubaker said.

Nato, Menowski, and Lewis joined them at the long table.

They ate quickly and silently, each man glancing to where Nolan lay a couple of tables away.

"Never thought I'd miss Iraq," Brubaker said, staring at his empty MRE container.

"Or Afghanistan," Caulfield added.

"Least we knew who our enemy was in those shitholes," Nato agreed.

"Never had to shoot another American," Menowski said.

"Those weren't Americans. Not anymore anyway," Lewis replied.

"Quit talking, all of you," Brubaker ordered. "We have a job to do. Let's do it."

"Sergeant Nolan got briefed after the last team came in. Do we know where we are going? What his orders were?" Lewis asked.

Brubaker stood up. "Don't you worry your pretty little head about it, Rifleman."

"What's that supposed to mean?" Lewis scowled.

"It means that with Nolan down, Brubaker is in charge," Nato said.

"Okay, but does he know shit?" Lewis asked.

"I know shit. Now get out there and sweep the rest of this level."

The squad checked their gear and weapons before leaving the mess room. Brubaker was the last to leave. He glanced back at Nolan, lying still on the table. He hoped there would be time to get him to safety.

CHAPTER 13

"Are they still out there?" Nicole asked.

After avoiding roaming packs of infected, they had taken refuge in another storeroom.

"No sign of them." Gretchen stood by the door of the dark storeroom. Bernard was sitting against the wall, eyes closed, breathing steadily. Michael was somewhere behind them, searching the shelves for anything useful.

"What's with you and Michael?" Gretchen asked without taking her eye away from the narrow gap in the open door.

"Nothing."

Gretchen glanced at Nicole. "You answered too quickly for it to be nothing."

"We were at a conference in Honolulu. I'd read some of his research, but never met him."

"He can be quite charming when he first meets a woman," Gretchen replied.

"There was a lot of drinking involved."

"There usually is."

"He cheated on you? While you were still together, I mean."

"Probably. When we first started dating and things got serious, he was doing his Master's in Marine Biology and I was working my ass off in the Navy. We didn't pay enough attention to each other to realize that a relationship was a bad idea."

"You got married; there must have been something between you."

"I guess."

Nicole shivered and hugged herself. "Look at us, two capable, professional women, completely failing at the Bechdel test."

"That's the movie thing, right?" Gretchen asked.

"Yeah, to pass the Bechdel test, two women in a film have to talk to each other about something other than a man."

Gretchen sighed. "I wish this was a movie; then we could leave the theatre early and get a coffee."

"And food, coffee and a bagel."

"I'll have a burger, chili fries, and a large coke." Gretchen grinned infectiously, which made Nicole giggle.

"What are you two talking about?" Michael emerged out of the darkness, looking intrigued and slightly nervous at the way the two women looked at each other and then giggled harder.

"Nothing. You want to wake up Bernard?" Gretchen asked.

"Hey, Bernard. Time to go." Michael nudged the scientist's foot. Bernard jerked awake with a snort.

"Whazzit?" he mumbled.

"We're moving out," Michael said.

"Okay…" Bernard blinked and worked himself off the floor. "I need to pee," he muttered.

"Back corner," Gretchen said. They waited in silence until Bernard returned.

"All set?" Michael asked. Bernard nodded and Gretchen opened the door.

Dark blood pooled along the hallway, streaked and smeared

where stumbling feet had dragged through the mess.

"There's an elevator over in section D-four," Gretchen said.

"And you're sure that we can access back-up data from the level three labs?"

"Nothing is certain," Gretchen replied.

"We should take the stairs." Bernard was on edge without the flamethrower to protect himself.

"Do what you want," Gretchen said. She glanced around the next corner and nodded it was all clear.

"These labs on level three?" Nicole asked. "What's the setup?"

"Biological specimen analysis. It's a secure level, so we have quarantine protocols and containment for anything pathological."

"Anything dangerous in there?"

Bernard stopped walking. "Smallpox, Ebola, and other genetically engineered variant strains of hemorrhagic fevers. Those are the ones I know about. Level three labs had things going on that they wouldn't even tell me about."

"If we can get in, maybe we can find some answers?" Michael suggested.

Gretchen nodded. "That's the plan. Maybe find out what's behind all this, and then we can take a sample back and that's our get out of jail free card."

Nicole stared. "You are seriously suggesting taking a potentially lethal unknown infectious agent out of a contained environment?"

"I'd rather get out alive and have something to guarantee our escape."

"Well, when whatever species evolves to take our place in the world millions of years from now, I hope they appreciate that you were the agent of their ascension," Nicole said.

Gretchen scowled. "Sure, maybe we can commission a fucking stone memorial somewhere when we get back to the mainland?"

Nicole's eyes narrowed. "I can't let you expose the rest of the world to an unknown infection."

A fit of coughing doubled Gretchen over. She spat blood leaned against the wall, struggling to breathe.

Michael immediately went to her side. "How are you doing?" She had been moving fast in spite of her wounded abdomen. He didn't know how she kept up the pace and intensity, but adrenaline was a great drug.

"I'm still here," Gretchen replied, her face pale and sheened with sweat.

Michael put a hand on her shoulder. "Nicole is right; we can't take a potentially lethal specimen out into the world. We need to know what it is and how it works."

"You need to get out of here. If you stay, you will die." Gretchen was almost pleading with him. Michael wasn't used to seeing her being vulnerable and he found himself unsure how to respond.

"I'll find a way."

Gretchen grimaced in pain. "If I don't make it, get out. Do whatever it takes."

"We're all getting out, I promise."

"You've made promises before." Gretchen winced as soon as she spoke.

Michael flinched like she had struck him. Standing up, he

walked to the next corner and checked the way to the elevator was clear.

They walked carefully, listening with each step for any sounds out of place. The corridors were strewn with debris, what might have been chunks of human flesh, and splashes of blood. Michael couldn't imagine how terrifying it must have been to be trapped in the facility when the shit really hit the fan.

Keeping up the pace, they made it to the elevator. Gretchen tapped the button and everyone stared at the metal doors, desperate for them to open, and at the same time, terrified of what might come out when they did.

"Fuck this, I'm taking the stairs." Bernard broke away and pushed the stairwell door open. Michael went to call after him, when the lift bell *dinged* and the mechanical doors slid open. Other than a bloody handprint smeared on the back wall and dried blood on the floor, the elevator was empty.

Further down the corridor, a low moaning sound rose and then they heard the slap of feet on the concrete floor.

"Go," Gretchen said.

They stepped in and she fumbled with an ID card, pressing it against a card reader until it beeped green and she tapped the button for level three.

Michael held his breath, the snarling breath of approaching infected getting louder and louder.

"Come on… Come on…" Nicole whispered. Shadows danced along the walls, and the smell of dried blood and shit washed over them. Gretchen tapped the close-door button repeatedly.

Filth-encrusted bodies lurched into view and swayed, looking for the source of the noise. They made eye contact with Nicole and awareness flared in their dark eyes. With a snort, one of the infected lunged forward, arms outstretched and slapping against the doors as they closed.

The closing doors hit the thrashing arms of the infected, and the lift doors opened like a can of sardines to starving cats.

Drooling mouths yawned wide, showing broken teeth and bloody gums. Gretchen stabbed at the nearest arm with the wooden stake she still carried. Michael and Nicole pressed back against the wall, kicking out at the reaching hands.

The press of snarling bodies was slowed down by the narrow space between the elevator doors. Nicole put a hand on Michael's shoulder and pushed herself up to stand on the handrail. Reaching above her head, she knocked a ceiling panel aside and peered up into the darkness of the lift shaft.

"We can get out this way!"

Gretchen and Michael ignored her, fighting against the oncoming horde with everything they could.

Without a useable weapon, Nicole jumped from the handrail and caught the edge of the ceiling frame. Her terror giving her strength, she pulled herself up, kicking her feet and waiting for one of the infected to grab her leg and drag her back down.

"Michael!" she yelled as soon as she was on top of the elevator. The biologist was covered in blood and gore as he wrestled and punched the hungry bodies reaching for him.

"Gretchen!" Nicole shouted. The Navy officer glanced up and nodded. "Michael, I'll hold them off. You get up there!"

Michael hesitated, a thousand reasons not to leave Gretchen behind paralyzing him.

"Fucking move!" his ex-wife yelled.

Michael jumped and grabbed Nicole's outstretched arm. Setting his feet on the rail, he pulled himself up through the hole.

Turning around, he stared down into the elevator. Gretchen was being overrun by the infected. Michael screamed her name and watched helplessly as Gretchen was dragged out of the elevator, vanishing under the snarling pile.

CHAPTER 14

"Climb!" Nicole shouted in Michael's ear. "We have to keep moving!"

Michael stood up, the space below their feet already filling up with more infected, reaching up to drag them down.

"Ladder," Nicole said and started climbing. She scampered up the narrow utility ladder, not looking back to confirm if Michael was following.

Numb with shock, Michael started climbing. The first set of elevator doors they passed was labeled LEVEL 6.

She kept climbing, feeling her way in the near-darkness until the next sign emerged; LEVEL 5.

"Level five!" she called down.

"We want level three," Michael replied.

Nicole rolled her eyes. "We're going the right way then."

With aching arms and sweat stinging her eyes, Nicole reached Level 3. She pressed herself against the side of the ladder and waited for Michael to climb up beside her.

"Think we should knock?" she asked. Michael just stared at her, his sense of humor taking a backseat to his shock and grief.

He reached up. "Grab the edge of the door, and I'll pull the other way; see if it opens."

They worked their fingers into the crack between the elevator doors and slowly separated them. The hallway on level 3 showed less signs of damage than the deeper level they had been through.

Nicole climbed over the threshold and crawled into the corridor. Around her, nothing moved, and she became aware of how bad she smelled with sweat, dirt, and blood staining her clothes and skin.

"It's clear," she whispered. Michael crawled out of the elevator shaft and slowly stood up next to her.

"Where's the lab?" he asked.

"Where's Bernard?" Nicole replied. "I guess we find the stairs and then find him."

Michael turned left and started walking. The corridor was lined with floor-to-ceiling windows. Most of the glass was covered with translucent film, hiding all but the strongest shadows from the well-lit rooms beyond.

The only labels on the glass doors were alphanumeric codes. Michael tried one of the doors and confirmed it was locked. A keypad on the side of each door needed an ID card and a PIN to access.

Nicole kept looking around, waiting for something to leap out at them, or for Bernard to show himself.

"Hey," Michael whispered. "I think I heard something."

Nicole froze, her ears straining, hearing nothing but her own heart thudding in her ears.

"Is that… music?" Michael turned slowly and started retracing his steps. They passed the elevator shaft and went to the far end of the corridor. The music was clearer here. It took a moment, but they both recognized the song from the hours of pop-radio play.

"I heard that the CIA uses music to torture people," Nicole

said softly.

"Listening to anything on constant repeat would drive me insane," Michael replied.

They tried the door where the music was loudest. "Hey, it's not locked," Michael whispered.

He pushed against the door, feeling whatever was barricading it slip on the floor. "Gimme a hand here."

Together, they pushed the door until it opened wide. The room beyond was a mess of empty cans, discarded MRE ration packs, and empty CD cases.

"Hello…?" Michael called.

"What if there are infected people in here?" Nicole whispered.

"Then we will bring them out into the open and deal with it."

Michael walked over to the stereo blasting out a Top 40 hit on repeat. Pressing the stop button, he almost shivered at the sudden silence.

"Hello?" he called again.

"Michael." Nicole had been exploring and held up a sheet of folded paper left on the laboratory bench. "It's a letter. Someone was here. A Marine called DeLuca. It says he went to search for survivors from his unit."

A thorough search of the three interconnected rooms revealed crates of military supplies, including ammunition and weapons. Food, water, and an insulated case with a biohazard symbol stamped on it. When Michael opened it, they found six thermos-like steel cylinders in their own individual slots. He picked each one up in turn and shook it gently. "I think these are empty."

"Do you think they knew what they were looking for?"

Michael shrugged. "They knew it was a biological agent." He

moved on to check another crate. It contained NBC kits; everything from hooded overalls to heavy-duty gasmasks and gloves. They were military-issue and another sign that the marines had some idea of what they were up against.

"Where the fuck is Bernard?" Nicole asked.

"I have no idea. You know how to handle a gun?" Michael asked.

"What? Not really. Do you?"

Michael shook his head. The crate of rifles and ammunition were tempting, and he wondered if he could work out the loading and safety and anything else required to shoot one.

"How hard can it be?" Nicole walked over and stared down at the rack of rifles in the open case.

"I think these are M16s. The US military has used them for decades because they're pretty simple."

"I thought you didn't know anything about guns?"

"Gretchen told me once. If she was here…" Michael trailed off and swallowed.

"I'm sorry," Nicole said.

"Fuck it." Michael lifted a rifle and took a full magazine from a second case. It took him a few attempts to slide it home. Once it clicked in place, he waited, as if expecting the rifle to start shooting without him touching the trigger.

"You have to cock it, that slide thing at the back. Pull it back," Nicole suggested.

Michael peered at the body of the rifle. He pushed a button in front of the trigger and the magazine dropped out and landed on the floor. "Shit."

Retrieving the magazine, Michael pushed it back into the gun and then slid the charging handle back. "Now what?"

"Let the slide thing go?" Nicole suggested.

The charging handle sprang back into the forward position. Michael turned the rifle over, making Nicole sway out of the path of the muzzle.

"Shit, the safety isn't on." Michael turned the rifle over and flicked the switch from the Fire position to the Safe position.

"Okay, I think it's ready," Michael said. He handed the rifle over to Nicole and repeated the clumsy process with a second one.

"Great. We are officially armed and dangerous. Are we going to shoot our way into the other labs?"

"Probably not a good idea. If they have infectious materials in them, we could risk flooding the entire facility with a super-flu or something worse."

"There is nothing in here that we can use," Nicole said. "We should have stayed put and waited for the marines to come back."

"We've come this far; we have to keep looking for answers."

"I'm not even sure what the damned question is!"

"You don't want to know what is causing this infection?"

"I don't care! I want to know why we were dragged out of a hotel in Hawaii and brought here. I want to know why someone deliberately killed the helicopter crew! I want to know why they sent us in here with only seven marines, especially after they had already sent in a team before and they never came back!"

"They might still be alive," Michael replied.

"Bullshit. Whatever this is about, anyone who knows anything is dead. We're going to die too. If not at the hands of those things, then the fucking government is going to shoot us for what we have seen."

"We get some answers, then they have to listen to us."

"Great. They can listen to us, then they can shoot us. It makes no difference to them."

"You're sounding paranoid," Michael said.

"It doesn't mean I'm wrong!"

Michael had no answer to that. As a scientist, he was intrigued by the potential of the facility and the specimens they may have discovered in the abyssal deep. As a person, he was terrified by what was happening around them.

Nicola took a deep breath. "I'm tired. I stink. I'm hungry."

"There's a bathroom, maybe a shower? There's spare clothes, in these crates. There's military rations in these boxes."

"Call for a pizza," Nicole said and closed the bathroom door behind her.

CHAPTER 15

Caulfield thumbed his radio. "Hey, Brew."

"Yeah?"

"Door on level five is shut tight."

"Locked?"

"No, I think it might be flooded."

"Hang on, I'm coming up."

Brubaker jogged up the final flight of stairs. The squad stepped aside and let him approach the door. He shone a light through the small window in the door, floating debris shining in the beam.

"Yeah, it's flooded."

The locking wheel on the door jerked and began to move, the bolts securing the door retracted as the wheel spun. Water gushed out as the locking pressure eased up around the rim.

"Shit, lock it up!" Brubaker yelled, straining to hold the turning wheel in place.

Lewis and Nato leaned on the wheel. It creaked and resisted their efforts. "Fucking thing won't close!" Nato replied. Lewis heaved on the wheel and swore loudly as it jerked from his grip and started to spin open.

"Someone's opening it from the other side!" Nato yelled.

"Move back!" Brubaker ordered.

The marines backed away, weapons raised. The water continued to gush, the torrent becoming a flood as the door opened wider.

"Level five is completely fucking flooded! How the fuck can someone be alive in there?" Caulfield shouted.

"Head upstairs!" Brubaker led his men up the stairs, the water roaring down the stairs behind them.

"It'll flood the levels below," Lewis warned.

"It depends," Nato replied. "If it's not coming in from anywhere, then sure. It'll drain down and maybe the pumps will take it out."

"If there's a breach somewhere and the water is getting in from the outside, then it's just going to keep on coming. The entire facility is going to be flooded."

"You are fucking kidding me?" Lewis replied.

"You got the map to this shithouse, don't you, Brubaker?"

"Yeah. I took it from Nolan. We keep going up. If four is flooded, we go to level three. Above that is just the power and air-supply systems. Other than the control room, no one is going to be up walking around in those utility tunnels. Too damned small."

"How much do we have to do to get the fuck out of here?" Menowski asked.

"We complete our sweep, find the sample containers, and set the timers for the shutdown procedure."

"Then we go home?"

"Then we go home."

"Fuckin' A."

A flashlight inspection through the porthole window in the level four door confirmed that this level was also flooded to the ceiling.

"How does that happen?" Caulfield asked.

"Sabotage?" Nolan suggested.

"Probably an emergency containment protocol."

"I thought these places were rigged with explosives and flammable gas?" Menowski replied."

"They are; that's the Death Valley Protocol for sterilization."

"Alpha team shut that down though, right?" Lewis asked.

"That's what we were told, yeah," Brubaker agreed.

"We gonna activate it again?" Nato asked.

"If we have to." Brubaker took the lead and headed up the stairs towards level three.

*

"Hey, at least there is no water on this level." Nato peered through the thick glass window into a dry corridor.

They cranked the door open and stepped out into a gleaming clean level three hallway. Glass and stainless steel shone, ready for inspection as if the horrors on the other levels had never happened.

"Hi, Honey, I'm home," Nato muttered.

Moving down the corridor in careful formation, the marines checked each of the glass doors as they passed. The card scanners all showed a red locked status, but they tried the doors anyway.

"All secure."

Brubaker paused at the last door on the right. The frosted glass made it impossible to see anything other than shadows inside the room. Someone moved in there.

With a gesture, Brubaker readied the squad for combat. They signaled they were ready and he jerked the door open.

"Whoa!" Michael threw his hands up as the marines burst into the room.

"What the fuck are you doing here?" Brubaker demanded. The squad spread out and checked the other rooms. Nicole screamed from the bathroom and they heard Lewis's mumbled apology as he backed out of the room and closed the door.

"She's, uhh, getting dressed," he said.

"After you left, we were attacked by infected."

"Where's the lieutenant and the others?"

"Gone," Michael said.

"If you had stayed where you were, they might still be alive. Did you think about that?" Brubaker asked.

"Fuck you," Michael snarled. "Gretchen was my wife."

"Ex-wife," Brubaker replied evenly. "You separated four months ago. Lieutenant Armitage took a posting here at that time."

"How the fuck do you know that?" Michael felt a cold child grip his spine.

"Nothing happens by coincidence, Doctor Armitage. You are here for a reason. Same as Doctor Saint-Clair. You were selected and brought along because the command structure has questions that they think you can answer."

"I'm a hydrozoan specialist. That's a type of jellyfish. I don't know shit about infectious disease."

"Maybe it isn't an infectious disease we are dealing with," Brubaker replied.

"It has to be, there's no..." Michael trailed off. "There was a jelly in the remains of a group of the infected. It had no place being there. I..."

"We have seen someone get infected. A blob of Jell-O, about the size of a fist, went into Sergeant Nolan's ear and seems to have taken up residence inside his head."

Michael laughed. "You are kidding me?"

Brubaker just stared at Michael, his face cold as stone.

"Holy shit… that's impossible. I mean, there's never been anything like that recorded or known to science."

"Well, if you can confirm what it is, maybe they will name it after you."

Michael shrugged. The idea of being published and famous, even in academic circles after this, seemed unlikely.

"Bernard, one of the onsite researchers, said that level three labs were where they kept all incoming specimens. He said whatever is going on, probably came from here."

"Is Doctor Saul also dead?" Brubaker asked.

"No, I mean, I don't think so? He was taking the stairs."

"We didn't see him, so he must be in here somewhere."

"We haven't been in any of the other labs. We don't have access."

Brubaker fished a plastic card out of his pocket. "This will get you into the other labs."

Michael took the tag and hesitated. "When we find a viable sample, what then?"

The marine medic regarded him steadily. "We go home, Doctor. All of us."

That same chill rippled down Michael's spine again. The door to the bathroom opened and Nicole stepped out, her wet hair slicked back and a military-issue jumpsuit hugging her body.

"Where's Sergeant Nolan?" she asked.

"He's doing his job, elsewhere," Brubaker replied. "If you have any questions, you can refer them to me."

"And will you answer our questions?"

"If I can." Brubaker smiled.

"Do you have any way of getting us into the secure labs on this level?"

Michael held up the plastic access card. "Already taken care of."

"Well, we should get on with it then."

The marines stood in silence while the scientists left the room. "Get me an inventory of this ordinance," Brubaker ordered.

*

"I guess we start with door number one," Michael said. He pressed the card against the sensor. It beeped twice and the LED switched from red to green. The magnetic locks clicked, and they pushed the door open.

"No pin code required?" Nicole said. "That's a pretty special access card."

"Lucky for us," Michael replied.

"Oh man... This is the kind of lab I dream of," Nicole said. Michael had to agree; the room gleamed with brand new equipment of all kinds. In a place like this, you could do chemical analysis, computer modeling, genetic manipulation to sample quarantine and containment from innocuous organisms to level four biohazards like weaponized smallpox.

A search of the room turned up nothing, except the airlock entrance to a higher-level hazard protection chamber.

Nicole opened a cabinet and removed a full-body pressurized suit. Slipping into it, she turned around so Michael could seal the suit and connect the air hoses. The suit inflated with filtered air, the pressure helping to minimize exposure to anything should the material get punctured.

Once Nicole gave him the thumbs up, Michael dressed in his own high-level protection. In ten minutes, they were both ready to pass through to the next room.

The pass card unlocked the door, and they went through the airlock.

Michael connected the air hose in the lab to his suit. Fresh, filtered air flowed over his face and he breathed slowly. The same tube had a communications cable attached. He connected Nicole to the same system.

"Can you hear me now?"

"Loud and clear."

They started the same search, examining liquid-filled containers of biological specimens and accessing computer log files after the white card gave access to the password locked terminals.

"Find anything?" Nicole asked after skimming through folders and files.

"Lots and lots of data, computer models of what I think are protein variants, and absolutely nothing that could be causing the kind of problems we are seeing."

Nicole came over and leaned in to review the screen. Even through the two atmospherically sealed suits, Michael imagined he could feel the heat of her body. The weird realization made him flush with guilt. Gretchen had just died. He shouldn't be feeling this way about someone he had only just met.

"It's a computer model all right. Genetic manipulation of proteins. Cheap food synthesis through rapidly growing base mediums."

"You can live on it, but it tastes like shit?" Michael suggested.

Nicole shrugged. "Add some chemical flavoring, it can be made to look and taste like anything."

"Nothing here to help us then." Michael turned his chair and stood up.

"Wait," Nicole called. "There's a reference to something called Project Galahad?"

"Does it say what Project Galahad is?"

Nicole remained silent as she clicked her way through the screens of data. "Holy shit…" she muttered.

"Found some crazy anime porn?" Michael asked.

"This has to be theoretical…" Nicole brought up another document, this one labelled TOP SECRET.

"Fine, theoretically speaking, what have you found?"

"Someone was doing a lot of very serious work on cellular immortality."

"Ha! That's hardly surprising. I mean, shit people have been looking into that since Paracelsus."

"Well, someone was making headway. They had isolated the genes responsible for cellular regeneration in *Turritopsis dohrnii.*"

"No shit?" Michael came back and pulled a second chair over to the screen.

"The Immortal Jellyfish," Michael said. "Technically, it's a hydrozoan, but they only live in the Mediterranean and off the coast of Japan."

"This is the result of genetic engineering. Michael, this is state of the art gene-manipulation. Someone has been splicing *Turritopsis* genes with human DNA."

"Well, that's bullshit. You may as well try and make a human-potato hybrid."

"We share at least twenty percent of our DNA with potatoes and a helluva lot more than that with jellyfish," Nicole said.

"It's still bullshit," Michael insisted.

"What if they found a species like *Turritopsis* and edited the gene sequencing on that?"

"They?" Michael looked at Nicole. "Excuse me, lady, your paranoia is showing."

"Fuck off," Nicole snapped. "Someone killed the helicopter crew and stopped them ever being able to report that we were dropped off next to a nuclear submarine! That's the *they* I'm talking about."

"Of course! The video, remember? Bernard said something about the Galahad Project not being affected by the weird shit going on?" Michael patted the inflated protective suit he was wearing.

"Shit, unplug me, quick."

"It might not be safe in here," Nicole warned.

"Fuck that, I found some papers; they're in my pocket."

Nicole unsealed Michael's suit and he emerged with a hissing of pressurized air. Digging in his jacket pocket, he pulled out the crumpled sheets of paper.

"Project Galahad," he said, holding them up.

Nicole took the paper and flicked through them. "Michael, this is half-burned, shredded, and the rest of it is blacked out. It doesn't tell us anything."

"Sure it does. It tells us that Project Galahad was top secret and someone tried to destroy documentation on it either before, or during, the current crisis."

"The current crisis? Is that what we're calling it now?"

"I don't know what we call it. But there's some shit going on here that goes beyond some kind of Ebola outbreak."

"Why us?" Nicole asked.

"Just lucky, I guess."

"Bullshit. Think about it. Your specialty is hydrozoans. Mine is genetic evolution. That Mister Suit guy, he knew what was going on here. He wanted us to come in and get data and get out alive."

"Then why did they try and kill us on the helicopter?" Michael finished stripping out of the hazard suit.

"Maybe we weren't the target?" Nicole swallowed hard. "The chopper went down after the sub was there to pick us up."

"Didn't that guy try and kill you?"

"I… I think so? He shot the pilots and then I stabbed him with a knife."

"Well, if we ever get out of here, we can ask Mister Suit what his evil plan was."

"Can we check the next lab?" Nicole asked.

Michael disconnected Nicole's suit and went out through the airlock. Nicole unsealed the bulky hood of her suit and pushed it back.

"May as well keep your suit on and go through to the next lab," Michael said.

"That is an awful breach of every safety protocol I have ever known."

"I agree, but right now, I don't think we have the luxury of time."

Without further comment, Nicole followed Michael through

the lab and out into the hallway. They entered the second lab. This one showed signs of live animal research. Aquarium tanks filled with frogs, fish, crustaceans, and mollusks lined the walls. The briny smell of sea water lay heavy on the air, and the brisk bubbling of air pumps oxygenating the water made the room hum.

Michael inhaled and grinned. This was his environment. The hiss and bubble, the silent lives of a hundred specimens from a dozen environments all living in close proximity, the secrets of their lives finally able to be observed and documented.

Nicole turned in a full circle around the room. "We don't even know what we are looking for."

"Brubaker, the marine? He said his men saw a jellyfish crawl inside Nolan's head."

"They saw what?" Nicole stared at him.

"A jelly, or hydrozoan, crawled into Nolan's head. Through his ear, or up his nose or something. I suggest we start looking for any signs of jellys."

"Jellyfish do not crawl inside people's heads!" Nicole laughed in a shrill sound at the lunacy of what Michael was suggesting.

"Oh come on! You've studied evolution at a genetic level. You know more than anyone here how minute changes in DNA can lead to abrupt changes in species. There could be any number of unknown species at depth. We just have to see what they brought on board and what they did with it."

Nicole turned away. "Fine. I'll check the computers, you check the tanks."

Michael started with the first aquarium. It was a tightly sealed Perspex tank, a gauge on the outside confirmed the pressure was set to match a depth of 12,000 feet. The creatures that swam, crawled, and waved, blind and colorless. They came from a world without light, where energy was limited, so they had adapted to drifting, or sitting and waiting for energy in the form of food to come drifting past.

No jellyfish, Michael confirmed after a minute of staring into the still waters.

He moved on to the next tank, sealed and pressurized for a depth of 15,000 feet. The pressure at that depth would be unimaginable, and yet, based on the samples in the tank, life thrived down there. Michael watched, fascinated as a pale anemone the size of a football dragged a transparent fish marked with flickering dots of luminescence into the fleshy sphincter of its mouth.

Moving around the tank, Michael heard water splash under his boots. He looked down at a spreading pool of cold sea water. A small tank of thick Perspex had cracked, releasing water onto the floor. A plastic tag still hung from one of the locking bolts on the container. *PROJECT GALAHAD. Hydrozoa. Species: Unknown. Dive: G36A7 Depth: 30,000 feet.* The date had been recorded too, but the writing had smudged too much to be legible.

"Hey," Michael and Nicole both said at once.

"I found something," they both spoke again.

"Quit repeating everything I say, and get your ass over here!" Nicole scolded.

Michael gave up and returned to where she sat in front of a computer screen.

"Ten days ago, a remote submarine dived to thirty-thousand feet, nearly to the bottom of the trench. It collected mineral, biological, and plant samples. The onboard computer recorded collection of what was identified as a snailfish specimen at twenty-eight thousand feet. Specimen was captured alive and secured in pressurized tank for return to the facility along with other specimens collected."

Michael frowned. "That can't be right. There's fuck-all life below twenty-thousand feet. It's beyond the Hadal Zone."

"Well, the team who identified the fish were surprised too. They decided it might be a new subspecies."

"Snailfish don't do the shit we have seen," Michael said.

"There is more," Nicole said, irritated at Michael's stating of the obvious.

"The snailfish was transferred to a holding tank, with pressure set at the maximum possible. The fish seemed to be fine. It ate, swam around, and generally did fish stuff."

"Fish stuff? Is that in the report?"

"No." Nicole waved a gloved hand. "You can read all the technical observations on your own time. There's hours of regular observations and it's all the same; fish stuff."

"Sure, fish stuff. What else?"

"Ahh… the specimen died two days after being put into the tank."

"That's it?"

"No. Christ, Michael, you really need to learn to shut up and listen."

Michael gritted his teeth. They needed answers and the methodical approach Nicole was taking to sharing what she had found was driving him nuts.

"The rest of the log is deleted. The login that deleted the remaining information was Doctor Bernard Saul."

"Hey, is there anything there about Project Galahad?"

The lights flickered for a moment and then the power went off, plunging the room into darkness. The air pumps whirred to a halt, and the only sound was the steady dripping of water.

"Still have your flashlight?" Michael asked.

"No, I think I dropped it."

"I lost mine too. The emergency lights should come on again in a second."

"The marines will be here before then…" Nicole found herself whispering in the darkness and shivered.

"You cold?" Michael asked.

"Cold and terrified," Nicole admitted.

"Me too," Michael said. "Okay, more terrified than cold."

Michael slipped his arms around Nicole, the hazmat suits she still wore crackling as the plastic crushed between them.

After a moment, Nicole felt a warm drip on her neck. "Are you okay?"

Michael made a wet sniffling noise. "Yeah, just ahh, shit. Just thinking about Gretchen all of a sudden." He pulled away, wiping his eyes and blinking away his sudden tears.

"Crying is normal. Screaming, curling up in a fetal position and howling like a wolf would also be completely normal. A person you loved just died. If that had happened to me, I'd be a complete wreck."

"I keep seeing it…" Michael whispered, the cracks in his voice clear in the darkness. "She looked at me when I was pulling you up through the hatch. She looked me right in the eye. She'd made her decision. She was going to sacrifice herself to save us."

"She was incredibly courageous," Nicole said softly.

"Who the fuck does that?" Michael's grief burst out in anger. "It's the kind of thing you see in movies. Some hero sends the others on while he stays behind, wounded with fuck all ammunition and he dies, but the chosen few get home because of it."

"Life is stranger than fiction," Nicole offered. "Sometimes, people do things we would never expect. Gretchen gave us the time to escape. She saved our lives. Now we have to find a way out of here and make sure she didn't die for nothing."

"Ha." Michael wiped his face with his sleeves and stood up. "With inspirational speeches like that, you should be coaching baseball. Little League, anyway."

Nicole smiled. Sitting there in the dark, with death and horror all around them, she almost giggled. It felt strangely cathartic, or an admission of insanity.

CHAPTER 16

"We got eight M16A2s, hundred rounds for each, in twenty-round mags. Two M911s, two spare mags for each. Four MPs, six mags each, and a Mossberg, with about thirty cartridges."

"Alpha team was prepared for anything. So why did they leave their extra ordinance here?" Lewis asked.

"I'd say they arrived, confirmed that everything was secure, placed their gear in a secure location, and went on to complete their mission."

"They didn't leave anyone on guard?" Nato looked around the room once again, as if checking to see if he had missed an extra marine.

"They would have. My guess is he got called up to action. No other reason to leave his post."

"Ooh rah!" the squad echoed.

"Lock this stuff away, secure the room, and on me." Brubaker checked his rifle and moved to the door. When the room plunged into darkness, Brubaker clicked on the lamp attached to his helmet. "We good?"

"Aye," the squad replied. The shadows fled as each man clicked the lamp on his helmet or flashlight on his rifle.

"Utility pipes should be secure against flooding," Nato observed. "If the place is flooding, it shouldn't affect the lights."

"Roger that," Brubaker agreed. "Someone's fucking with us. Let's go, Marines."

In formation, they exited the room, beams of light sweeping the hallway and reflecting off the frosted windows of the labs.

"The squints should be behind one of these unlocked doors. Find them and keep sharp."

The marines paired off, and in less than a minute, they found the two civilians.

"The lights went out," Michael said, shading his eyes against the bright beams of the headlamps.

"No shit?" Menowski replied.

"Any idea why?" Michael asked, ignoring the sarcasm.

"I suspect sabotage," Brubaker said. "The power generators are robust and have backup systems for their backup systems. Without electricity, there's no air recycling. Without air, we all die."

"We found some stuff on the computer," Nicole announced. "Logs from a remote sub dive. They found some weird shit and there was an accident. After that, the logs were wiped by Bernard."

"Define weird shit," Brubaker replied.

"A snailfish; a known species of the Kermadec Trench, except this one shows up at an impossible depth. It's alive and is captured by the specimen collector tools on the sub. They bring it back here and it gets observed for a couple of days. Then it died and something happened. We don't know exactly what happened because the logs were deleted. Now that the power is out, we may never know."

"Did something come out of this snail and eat someone's brain?" Brubaker asked.

"Snail*fish*. It's not a gastropod, it's a fish," Michael said.

"We don't know if something came out of it and did… that," Nicole said over Michael before one of the marines decided to slap him.

"Well, we haven't seen any fish crawling around," Nato said.

"Wait." Michael put a hand to his head as if bracing himself against an idea. "The jellyfish, or hydrozoan, or bacterium, or worm, or whatever the fuck it is, was in the snailfish. Maybe the parasite organism takes over the nervous system and piggybacks a ride with the host? It forces a snailfish out of its usual extreme habitat and makes it swim deeper. The host dies, maybe as part of the parasite's lifecycle? This thing which seems to be able to survive some really shitty environmental conditions, somehow breaks out of the holding tank, and then what? Crawls around until it finds a new host?"

"If the death of the host was part of the organism's life cycle, it might have spawned in the fish?" Brubaker suggested.

"That could explain the rapid spread," Nicole said. "Or, this thing can reproduce in a living organism and has the awareness to wait until the best circumstances for survival exist before spreading."

"Twenty-four hours," Michael said. "The first reports of people disappearing, they were gone for less than twenty-four hours. Maybe that is how long it takes for the organism to get control?"

"Nolan," Brubaker said. "When this thing got in Nolan's head, it knocked him out cold."

"He had some kinda fit first," Lewis said. "Like my cousin, when he sees a flashing light."

"That would suggest a serious brain trauma," Brubaker replied.

Nicole wrapped her arms around herself. "For twenty-four hours, it grows inside the host? Then they wake up and go nuts?"

"The report we saw said that when the infected turned up again, they seemed a bit confused, strange but not violent. Cross didn't go kill-crazy," Michael replied. "And who was that other woman? Naki-something?"

"Chief Medical Officer, Doctor Kimo Nakiro?" Brubaker asked.

"Yeah, Bernard said she vanished, then when she showed up again, she told him everything was fine."

"What are the common factors?" Nicole stripped the gloves off her hazmat suit and marked her points on her fingers.

"Females don't go insane? Any correlation between age, ethnicity, medical history… ah, food allergies? Time spent on the facility? Contact with a human host prior to their own infection?"

"Maybe they pass it on by fucking?" Caulfield said, looking up from where he was cleaning his fingernails.

Lewis laughed and even Nato grinned.

"It's entirely possible," Nicole said, completely serious. "Exchange of body fluids, or sexual fluids – that's cum and pussy juice to you, Marine – could be a transmission vector."

Lewis sniggered and the others just stared.

"We don't know anything," Michael said.

"Come on, Michael, we're scientists. Think about what we have seen. This parasite enters a new host, and for the first twenty-four hours, the infected host is in a coma, or driven to hide itself while the organism takes control. Once control is established, it then goes in search of what, other potential hosts?"

"That makes sense. The basic instinct of all life forms is to survive and reproduce."

"Right, so once it walks into a group of people all camouflaged as one of them, it passes something on to the next individual. Either some kind of offspring, or larval stage, or eggs, then it repeats the cycle..."

"What about the ones that died?" Michael asked.

"Failed to gain control over the host organism?" Nicole said. "The parasite couldn't take them over sufficiently, but it did enough damage to kill them?"

"Shit..." Michael trailed off. "That would make sense. Think about it. If you are a species that survives by taking control of a host's central nervous system – easy enough in your average fish – then you encounter something far more complex in a human brain. There's a high chance of doing serious damage and killing the host."

"Or driving them insane..." Nicole said quietly. "The infected. All those people? What if they have this hydrozoan in their heads, but the damage is too great. They've lost all cognition and are operating on basic instincts of fight and feed?"

"What about, the need to fuck?" Lewis grinned.

"In higher-functioning organisms, sexual drive is a very strong instinct. This is a creature that probably produces in a different way, inside the host body."

"Makes sense; bunch of squints down here wouldn't be fucking each other anyway."

"Lewis, go stand sentry in the hallway until relieved," Brubaker ordered. Lewis looked ready to object and then stomped out of the room.

"Now we need to know how to contain one of these fucking things and destroy everything else," Nato spoke up.

"Fuckin' A," Menowski agreed.

"What else we got?" Brubaker asked.

"A whole lot of questions and fuck-all answers," Michael replied.

Muffled shouting interrupted the meeting; Lewis barking orders and the ominous sound of his rifle being readied to fire.

The marine squad took up defensive positions, ready to tear up the place on Brubaker's orders.

"Brubaker, coming out!" he yelled.

"I'm not infected! I'm not infected!" a voice yelled, shrill with fear.

"Bernard?" Michael said.

"Where the fuck has he been?" Nicole replied and they ran for the corridor.

"Squints coming in!" Caulfield yelled before Lewis or Brubaker could shoot them for coming up announced.

"Bernard? Where the hell have you been?" Michael shouted.

"I thought I heard some of those things coming... I locked myself in a lab store room and..." the scientist trailed off and shrugged.

"You're okay though, right?" Nicole asked.

"Yeah, I'm good." Bernard looked concerned at the filthy marines standing in the pristine surroundings of the secure laboratory level.

"We have a theory," Michael grinned, "about the source of infection, the transmission vectors, and why so many of the base inhabitants went completely fucking psychotic."

"Oh… good."

Bernard listened while Michael and Nicole explained what they had found, but neither of them mentioned the missing log files deleted with his authorization.

"It is a hydrozoan? Do you have a viable sample?" Bernard asked when they were done.

Nicole shook her head. "Not yet, but they shouldn't be too hard to find. Sergeant Nolan was infected. He's secure on one of the lower levels."

Brubaker stepped forward. "You're the only survivor of the original staff?"

"Yes," Bernard replied.

"What happened to Hayley Cross? She was with you when we left?" Brubaker asked.

"We left her behind. She was infected," Michael said.

"Where's Gretchen?" Bernard asked.

"She didn't make it." To Michael, it felt like the words were coming out of someone else's mouth.

"Are there any of these fucking jellyfish still in containment?" Brubaker asked.

"No," Bernard replied. "I mean, we didn't know they existed. So they wouldn't be in containment."

Michael opened his mouth to ask him about the label on the breached Perspex holding tank, then closed it again.

"Well, I'm glad you're okay, Bernard." Nicole gave the scientist a quick smile, which made him blush again.

"Hey, Brubaker, you read much?" Michael asked casually.

"What? Sure, I guess. Why, you wanna start a book club?"

"Sure, what else are we going to do down here? I was just thinking about the classics. You know like, King Arthur and the Knights of the Round Table."

"Yeah, I think I saw the cartoon with the sword in the stone when I was a kid."

"Right… In Arthurian legend, the greatest quest they went on was the search for the Holy Grail."

"The cup that Christ drank from at the Last Supper?" Brubaker asked.

"If you like," Michael replied. "Anyway, the cool thing about the Arthurian legend was that three of Arthur's knights actually found the grail. The greatest treasure imaginable, and they actually found it."

"Yeah, that Indiana Jones movie, right?"

"Not a big reader I take it?" Bernard asked.

"Comic books and enough medical textbooks to get me through specialist medic training. What's your fucking point?"

"Nothing," Bernard said quickly, the smirk vanishing from his face.

"Armitage, if you have a point, I suggest you start running until you reach it," Brubaker said.

"Of the three knights who found the Holy Grail, only one of them received its greatest gift: immortality. This knight's name was Sir Galahad."

"Well, shit, I am so glad you felt this was important enough to give a lecture on right here and now."

"Bernard," Michael turned and smiled at the scientist, "what the fuck is Project Galahad?"

CHAPTER 17

"I-I don't know," Bernard stammered.

"Okay, try this one: ever heard of *Turritopsis dohrnii*? Commonly known as the Immortal Jellyfish?"

Bernard shook his head, his gaze skittering across the floor.

"Maybe it's just coincidence, but maybe it isn't. Galahad, the immortal knight, an unknown species of hydrozoa that might be infecting human hosts, and a species of hydrozoa that is functionally immortal?"

"You cannot seriously be suggesting they are somehow connected?" Bernard tried to laugh and made a wheezing hiccup sound instead.

Michael laughed. "Of course not. I'm just fucking with you, man. But seriously, what is Project Galahad?"

"I don't know. I have never heard of it," Bernard said, his voice cracking dry.

"Doctor Bernard Saul? Head of research at a top-secret facility dedicated to military research and there's an entire project going on that you don't even know about?" Michael kept smiling, but his voice was getting colder.

"What is he talking about, Saul?" Brubaker asked.

"I honestly have no idea. There were so many projects going on here. I didn't have access to a lot of the files. People came in, they did their work, they left again, and they took their data with them."

"Like the cockroach astronaut guy?" Nicole suggested. "You knew all about that project. How could you not know?"

"Information is compartmentalized," Bernard explained. "We are only told what we need to know. No one knows everything; it's a security protocol."

Michael exploded in Bernard's face. "Goddamnit, Bernard, you deleted log files relating to the snailfish specimen! The same specimen that was collected on the final dive before this place started turning to shit!"

"I had no choice!" Bernard wailed.

"Why did you delete the log files?" Michael continued his verbal assault.

"I had no choice!" Bernard yelled again.

"Project Galahad, Bernard. Someone is blending hydrozoan and human DNA. What do you know about it? Maybe something got out of the lab? A specimen that breached quarantine? Maybe it's what is infecting everyone? Got any ideas on that Bernard?"

Bernard shook his head.

"Fuck this. Brubaker, you can shoot him without killing him, right?" Michael stepped out of the way.

"Fuckin' A," Brubaker leveled his rifle at the trembling Bernard.

"Wait, this is insane, Michael!" Nicole grabbed his arm when she realized he and Brubaker were serious.

"What do we need to access Saul's files?" Michael asked.

"Log in and password?" Brubaker replied.

"This skeleton key card you have, it can access all the

systems?"

"Yeah, it's supposed to."

"Okay, we can use it to bring up everything that Bernard Saul has accessed. Project files, dive-mission logs, even facility life support systems and power controls."

Bernard's cheek twitched. "You have no right. You are not authorized."

"It would be easier if you just tell us what you know, Bernard," Nicole said. "We just want to find the truth and get out of here."

"Truth?" Bernard smiled, his lips curling back over his teeth. "You have no comprehension of the truth."

"Explain it to me like I'm five," Michael said.

"It isn't that simple. It was never meant to be like this. Look, genetic engineering of hydrozoan DNA with human stem cells has been an ongoing project here for some time. I can't even begin to tell you where our funding comes from. It's higher than federal. It's beyond black-book."

"No shit," Michael replied. "How are Project Galahad and our current shit storm related?"

"I honestly don't know," Bernard insisted. "Galahad is a successful project. We... we were initiating the next stage of testing when the outbreak of whatever this infection is happened."

"We know what the fucking infection is," Brubaker interrupted. "It's fucking jellyfish getting in people's brains and fucking them up!"

"It's unfortunate," Bernard agreed. "Gretchen recommended you be brought in, Michael. She said even though you were an asshole, you were the best person to join the team for the next phase."

"What is the next phase?"

"Human testing," Nicole whispered. "Human testing, right?"

"Jesus Christ. You injected this Frankenstein DNA into humans?" Michael asked.

"Yes," Bernard raised his hands as Brubaker lifted his rifle and made ready to smash the scientist's face in, "but those people are fine! They're not infected!"

"Bullshit!" Brubaker snarled.

"The modified DNA! It protected the test subjects from the parasite. We don't know why, or how it works, but the invasive species doesn't attempt to assimilate with a genetically modified host!"

"The test subjects? Who are they?" Nicole stared at Bernard, a grim realization apparent on her face.

Bernard's lips peeled back in a grin and then retracted over his gums until the skin of his face started to distort. Teeth dripped from his gaping mouth like shards of melting snow falling from the eaves of a rotted mountain cabin.

"The fuck…?" Michael backed away, grabbing Nicole by the arm and pulling her with him.

The flesh of Bernard's mouth split open and a spaghetti bowls' worth of glistening tendrils rose out of his throat and probed the air. Brubaker lifted his rifle and fired a three-round burst into Bernard's face. Cracks spread from the bullet entry points in his forehead and cheek. The skin swelled and split until chunks of Bernard's head fell away like a shattered ceramic mask.

The other marines charged forward as Brubaker retreated, continuing to fire into the expanding mass that tore its way out of

Bernard's body.

Michael and Nicole ducked for cover, crawling away from the firestorm erupting behind them. Bernard's skin tore and vomited out grey jelly, a man-sized form rising from the steaming carcass it shed.

Rifle rounds burst into the shapeless form with no sign of serious injury. Thin tentacles emerged from the translucent wet skirt that quivered against the floor. The thing moved towards the marines. More tentacles sprang from what was left of Bernard's throat. They whipped through the air, slapping against the glass walls and striking Caulfield across the face.

The rifleman screamed, a red welt blistering on his cheek where he had been struck. The others maintained a steady rate of fire.

"Rifles fire is ineffective!" Brubaker yelled. "Pull back!" He grabbed Caulfield by the back of his vest and dragged him down the hall.

Gunfire continued as the squad fell back. Lewis ducked into the room where the rest of their weapons were still waiting. He grabbed the Mossberg shotgun and loaded it with shaking hands.

Racking the slide, he ducked out again, stepping around Brubaker and the stumbling Caulfield, whose face had turned purple and swollen beyond recognition.

Sighting down the center of the corridor, Lewis fired the shotgun. It boomed, and the tight spread of buckshot tore a massive hole in the advancing monster.

"Suck this, you shit-fucker!" Lewis roared and fired again. Wet chunks of gel splattered against the glass walls and the whip-like tendrils lashed out again, striking against Lewis' helmet and filling his nostrils with the sharp stink of acidic venom. He fired again, each shot blasting into the pulsing form.

Nato stepped up with an MP5 and emptied it in a single burst. The man-sized lump of pulsing jelly came apart in a wet blast of chunks.

"Holy fucking shit..." Lewis breathed. "That is some seriously fucked-up shit."

"Keep away from it!" Brubaker yelled from the storeroom doorway. "Squints! Get your asses in here!"

Nicole broke away from Michael and ran. Brubaker guided her through the doorway and then covered the others as they completed their retreat.

"Is it dead?" Nato asked.

"Yes, I mean, I think so," Michael replied. "It came apart; it has to be dead."

"The fuck is that shit? I mean, that's some fucking sci-fi channel shit," Nato sputtered, trying to catch his breath.

"Now you freak out?" Michael stared at him. "Jesus Christ..."

"If it's dead, we can get some samples," Nicole said. She tore open the biohazard container and started pulling out the flasks.

Caulfield started convulsing. Brubaker went to his side and held him down. "Menowski! Help me here!"

Menowski slung his rifle and grabbed Caulfield by the shoulders while Brubaker injected the spasming marine with an emergency syringe.

"He's not breathing!" Menowski yelled.

Brubaker pressed his fingers against the swollen mass of Caulfield's neck. "Open his shirt!"

The medic stabbed Caulfield in the chest with an epinephrine shot, injecting adrenaline straight into his heart.

"Starting compressions," Brubaker announced and began rhythmically pushing on Caulfield's chest.

"What can we do?" Nicole asked, pushing past Menowski.

"Back off," the marine snapped. "Let Brew do his job!"

"Nicole, we'll collect those samples," Michael said.

The corridor stank of brine and acrid chemicals. They carefully scraped lumps of the jelly into the containers and sealed them tight.

"I hope this is enough," Nicole said.

"Project Galahad…" Michael muttered. "What the hell were they thinking?"

"Human immortality." Gretchen stepped out of the darkness, her naked body shimmering like liquid diamond.

CHAPTER 18

"Gretchen?" Michael just about whooped in surprised delight. "You're–" he wanted to say *alive!* and in a sense, she was. Alive, but no longer human.

"Project Galahad. Years of experimentation, analysis, and finally a break through. Serendipity they call it."

"An accident that has a beneficial outcome," Michael interrupted.

"Always so eager to explain, Michael. Always talking over others, arrogantly proving your greater knowledge and your greater worth."

"My worth isn't that great. I have credit card debt and I'm all out of research grant funds."

"The immortality of certain hydrozoans has been known. The Japanese research proved it in a laboratory environment. Yet, the focus has always been on the genetic manipulation of human stem cells. I am proof that there is a better way."

"You're a walking Jell-O mold," Nicole snapped.

"I am undergoing a metamorphosis. The butterfly becomes the larvae, and then a butterfly again."

"You hate bugs," Michael replied, slowly backing away with Nicole behind him.

"It feels incredible, Michael. You can be part of the next stage of human evolution. Stay with me; your expertise in hydrozoan biology will be an asset to our ongoing research program."

"You are offering me a job, even now?"

"Of course, why else would you have been brought here?"

"We were told there was some kind of accident, a problem that needed our… Oh…" Nicole went pale.

"Nicole Saint-Clair, world authority on evolutionary genetics. Who better to guide Michael through the delicate forest of rapidly evolving DNA?"

"You and Mister Suit arranged all this? You brought us here to work on this insanity?"

"Regrettably, before you arrived, a new species of hydrozoan was collected and it proved to be difficult to contain. Saul went rogue and contacted our command structure. They arranged for the Navy to send in armed marines. This new hydrozoan showed a remarkable ability to infiltrate and control the human nervous system. This integration was not always successful and there were casualties, which accelerated the breakdown of less suitable specimens."

"You mean, people. You are talking about people," Michael replied.

"Some died; others were damaged beyond repair. We needed to maintain control of the facility until you arrived. Now you are here, and you will join us. This species was an unexpected interruption to the research program. However, you are here now, and we will regain control."

Nicole had reached the door. She raised her voice, hoping to alert the marines inside. "I have to say, Gretchen, for someone who is infected, your plan has some serious flaws!"

Shadows moved on the other side of the frosted glass. Nicole tensed, glancing towards Michael, who nodded slightly. They threw themselves flat and the glass wall exploded in a storm of MP5 rounds.

Gretchen shrieked and bolted into the darkness down the hallway. The marines came through the shattered wall and checked on the civilians.

"My ex-wife," Michael managed. "She's like the queen bitch jellyfish."

"Yeah, I was married once," Nato replied.

Nicole lifted her head from the floor. "We got the samples. Can we destroy this place and get out in time?"

Nato thought for a moment. "Brubaker has the Death Valley activation codes. We need to have a way out first."

"Easy. We go back down to level seven and you guys can contact the submarine and we walk out of here." Nicole climbed to her feet.

"Caulfield's gone," Brubaker said, stepping into the ringed circle of flashlight beams.

"Ooh rah," Menowski murmured.

"We might not be able to get back to the sub," Nato continued. "Levels four and five are flooded, and if they have been breached, the pumps are offline until we can get the power back on. Even then…"

"Why can't we just talk to the sub?" Michael asked. "Get them on the radio or something?"

"Communications went down fifteen minutes after the first fire-team came in. We never heard from them again," Brubaker said.

"There must be a contingency plan? You have a way of contacting the sub, right?" Nicola asked.

"Communications in a structure like this are complicated. Radio signals don't penetrate. Wired communications work fine, but they've been offline since before we arrived."

"What was your plan? Once you completed your mission?" Michael asked.

Brubaker sighed. "Walk out the way we came in. If the flooding can't be controlled, then we are not going to be able to do that. There are other ways out."

"Other ways out?" Nicole prompted.

"Emergency egress, life boats if you like. They are emergency submersibles that have limited range and function, but in a pinch will allow you to move around outside the facility."

"Will they get us to the surface?"

"No way in Hell. You would need to depressurize for days, and the air-cleaning systems, not to mention the batteries, would never survive long enough for you to reach the surface. If something went wrong and you came up too fast, you'd die pretty damn quickly."

"Okay," Michael said. "We take our samples, check if the lower levels are still accessible, and then we get out and get the mother ship to come and pick us up. Easy."

Brubaker didn't look convinced, but he nodded. "Nato, with me. We're going down to level seven to asses flooding. If that's all good, we log in and start the Death Valley Protocol. Then, we go home."

"Ooh rah!" Menowski and Lewis chanted.

CHAPTER 19

The noise of the water flooding down the stairwell from level four was deafening.

Nato leaned in and yelled to be heard, "With the power out, we have no pumps!"

"The backup generators are designed to be a failsafe!" Brubaker shouted.

"Yeah, but they only work if they know the power system is down. If the computer was messed with, it might have never activated the backup systems."

"Can we fix it?" Brubaker shouted.

"I dunno." Nato didn't like to make promises.

Brubaker went back to staring at the open door that led to level four. The volume of water pouring through the gap meant that they had a leak somewhere in that level. This was fresh sea water. The entire Pacific Ocean was coming in, and it would keep coming in until the entire base was flooded. "No sign of any infected. If we can get that door closed, we'll head up to the utilities control on level two! See if we can't get the pumps back on line!"

Nato nodded, and they warily stepped down into the freezing water. With each step, it rose over their boots and then swirled around their knees. At the landing, the water was thigh deep and close to freezing.

Both marines scanned their surroundings constantly. A battle-honed awareness of danger kept them on edge and ready to react without thinking. Nato reached the door first and started to push. The water pouring through carried tons of weight with it. Brubaker took a last glance around and then joined Nato in pushing against the flood.

A hand of swollen flesh, wrinkled and grey from long exposure to the water, curled around the door from the other side.

"Fuck!" Brubaker shouted. "Too much water coming through!"

Gesturing to Nato, they stepped back and retreated up the stairs as the rising water followed their boots. An infected man squeezed through the gap, his water-logged skin peeling like old wallpaper as it tore against the steel of the half-open door.

Nato opened fire. His first round ricocheted off the bulkhead and went into the water. The second shot shattered the infected man's nose and tore a chunk out of the back of his skull.

They didn't have to wait long for more infected to reach the door. The strong current swept them off their feet and they piled up against the door. Writhing and slithering over each other, they struggled to get through.

"Maybe they will dam up the flow?" Nato shouted.

"I'm not sure we could be that fucking lucky!"

*

"Now the rifle is loaded, and you can click the safety from fire to safe," Menowski instructed the two scientists. "Always treat a firearm as if it were loaded. Never pick one up unless you are prepared to fire it. These are military-issue M16A2s; you have an extra setting for full automatic that you don't find on civilian assault rifles. Do not turn the fire selector to full automatic. You will just be wasting ammunition."

The marine unloaded the rifle, his movements almost a blur. "Any questions?"

Nicole and Michael hesitated. "Could you run through that one more time?" Michael asked.

Menowski started again from the beginning, identifying the parts of the rifle, the ways it came together, and the key steps to loading and readying it to fire.

The scientists were working through the steps on their own when Nato and Brubaker came back from their trip to the lower levels.

"No sign of your ex-wife," Brubaker said before Michael could ask. "Okay, listen up. The pumps are out with the power being down. The backup generators are offline. We need to find out why. Nato and I are going up to the utility control room on level two, see if we can get the pumps online."

"How can we help?" Nicole asked.

"Are you an engineer? Mechanical? Electrical? Computer technician?" Brubaker asked.

"I can change the oil in my car," Nicola said.

Brubaker stifled a grin. "Well, I'll keep that in mind."

Michael swept a hand through his hair. "We can stay here and keep reviewing the paper files we found, see if we can learn anything else about this organism."

"Menowski, keep them safe. We will be back ASAP."

"Aye," Menowski replied. "All right, Squints. Let's get back to rifle drills."

*

At the top of the stairs leading to level two, a sign warned against unauthorized entry. It also declared that danger and high voltage were locked away behind the reinforced door.

The all-access pass card cleared the way, and the two marines stepped into a silent chamber lined with racks of high-capacity batteries.

"These are all charged at least… seventy percent," Nato said.

"Here's your problem." Brubaker crouched at a cable conduit in the floor. The plastic grille over the concrete trench had been forced up and the pipe underneath was hacked open.

"I've found the murder weapon," Nato announced, his flashlight catching the gleam of a discarded fire axe.

"Sonnovabitch," Brubaker muttered.

"If the generators are shut off, and the power cable to the batteries is cut, why didn't the backup generators kick in?" Nato asked.

"Because we are dealing with assholes," Brubaker said.

The continued their search of the room, passing the floor-to-ceiling shelves of batteries and coming to another door. Further warning labels reminded them that they had no right to be here, and proceeding past this point was not an option.

Brubaker's pass card worked its magic and the magnetic locks clicked open.

The smell of burned plastic and flesh stung their nostrils. "Something died in here," Brubaker said.

"Body, two o'clock," Nato replied.

The woman showed signs of electrical burns on her hands that had charred her fingers to blackened sticks. The scorch marks on her arms showed where the arcing current had rippled up her limbs until it fried her brain and set her hair on fire.

Brubaker nudged the body with his foot. "Dead," he confirmed and then dragged her out of the way.

"Maybe she tripped the circuit breakers?" Nato suggested. He pointed his flashlight towards a metal box on the wall; black scorch marks radiating out from it indicated an electrical explosion.

Brubaker opened the box, the smell of scorched insulation stronger now. "I hope this works." He flicked the first of five circuit breakers, and then when he didn't die, went on and reset the others.

"Well, that didn't work," Nato said.

Brubaker frowned and then pushed a large red button. A deep humming sound thrummed around them and the lights began to glow the color of concentrated piss.

They waited, watching the lights as the generators powered up and the light gained strength.

"Houston, we have lift-off," Brubaker said.

"If the connection to the batteries isn't fucked," Nato replied.

"Have faith, man."

"Never seen the point," Nato said.

In the battery room, rows of green LEDs were blinking as the cells sucked up the voltage flowing through them.

Tapping the keyboard on a console, Brubaker brought the screen to life. "Power's back on in all sections," he confirmed.

"Fuckin' A."

"Hey, there's security monitors here." Brubaker pulled out a chair and brought the screens online.

"Shit. Nothing," Brubaker said.

"Water must have shorted them out."

"I hope the pumps are working."

Nato nodded. "Ready to end this party?"

"Check." Brubaker dug in his fatigues and pulled out a red plastic card. Peeling a sticker off it, he bent the card until it cracked along a line. Pulling the two sections apart, Brubaker extracted a printed code.

Tapping on the computer terminal keyboard, he accessed the Death Valley Protocol screen. There were no instructions, no warnings; just a blinking cursor where the activation code could be entered. Taking a deep breath, Brubaker read off the card and typed with one finger. Sixteen characters. Then a second screen with an Activate Death Valley Protocol Yes or No button.

Brubaker clicked the "Yes" button firmly.

The screen now showed the following message, Death Valley Protocol activated. *30:00... 29:59... 29:58...*

"Thirty-minute countdown has been activated," Brubaker said.

Readying their rifles, the two marines left the utility control room and headed down past level three and on to level four.

The makeshift dam of squirming bodies had been eroded by the flood. A severed arm swirled in an eddy, bumping against glistening chunks of grey skin and meat. The water level was holding, but the levels below were fully flooded.

"Pumps aren't going to make enough of a difference if we can't close that door!" Brubaker yelled.

"We should just get the fuck out!" Nato yelled back.

Turning his back on the swirling water, Brubaker nodded. The power being back on was a step in the right direction, but they needed to leave the doomed facility before the countdown expired. "Back to Menowski and the squints!" he yelled.

A figure rose out of the dark water, torn marine fatigues hanging in strips from the body. It lunged and wrapped its arms around Brubaker's neck and chest. Heaving backwards, the infected marine sank his teeth into the medic's neck and they crashed down into the water as Nato opened fire, his shots striking the water in a row of sharp splashes.

"Brubaker!" he yelled. "Brew!"

Nato wavered, looking for any sign that the medic might resurface. After a couple of minutes of nothing but more grey flesh twisting on the current, he backed away up the stairs.

CHAPTER 20

"Menowski!" Nato announced his presence when he reached the level three corridor.

"Here!" Menowski replied, appearing out of the storeroom with his rifle casually ready. "Hey, where's Brew?"

"Infected got him. Brubaker's KIA."

"Fuck. Fuck. Fuck!" Menowski turned in a tight circle. "Well, that's just fucking great! What the fuck are we going to do now?"

"We are going to keep our shit together," Nato said firmly. "You're a marine, not a fucking pussy, and we are not done yet."

"Brew was good people," Menowski said.

"Ooh rah. Didn't your recruitment officer warn you that this job could get you killed?"

"Nah, that asshole said I would get a college education and a government pension."

"How are our civilians?"

"Armitage is taking a shower. The chick is having some chow."

"DVP is active. We have twenty minutes to get out."

"I'll tell the squints to stow their shit," Menowski replied.

Nato pulled out his copy of the facility map and ran his finger over it.

Behind manual bulkheads at various points, there were narrow shafts with ladders that could be sealed off at each level. The shafts connected to a series of sealed chambers where emergency submarines were supposed to be available to evacuate survivors.

It would be enough to get them back safely into the open water. Once they were outside the radio-signal-blocking shell of thick concrete, steel and stone, contacting the submarine for pickup would be easy.

Nato traced a short line from their current position to the nearest emergency egress shaft. It was time to put the plan into action. He walked into the room, where Michael was pulling on a shirt. "You got the pumps working?" the scientist asked.

"Yeah, but the water is coming in from the outside; we can't go out the way we came in."

"You found another way out?" Nicole swallowed the last mouthful of MRE and wiped her face.

"The emergency evacuation shafts with ladders in them. They connect to escape points, where, if our streak of good luck continues the way it has so far, will have deep sea mini-subs that we can use to get out into the open water. From there, we can contact the submarine and get picked up."

"Sounds good." Menowski fidgeted while the others gathered weapons and the limited supplies that Nato would let them take.

"Follow me." Nato led them to one of the labs where they moved a steel bench aside and he opened a panel marked, *Emergency Access Only.*

The rubber seal around the hatch stuck for a moment and then popped open. The smell of brine and stale air wafted out of the shaft. Nato swept the dark tunnel with a flashlight and declared it safe.

"I'll go first, then Saint-Clair, then Armitage. Menowski, you bring up the rear."

"Aye," Menowski replied.

Nato ducked through the square hole. The ladder was firmly bolted to the wall, and he locked his arm around a rung before looking down as far as the flashlight beam could reach.

The water twenty feet below was still and dark. The shaft would go as deep as the seventh level if the bulkheads were open, then the water would have gone all the way to the bottom.

"Stay close," Nato said to Michael, who was crouched at the hatch and waiting to follow him.

The marine climbed, and Michael stepped on to the ladder and started after him. Nicole tightened the straps on the rucksack she had stuffed with three of the specimen containers and crawled through the hatch.

With Michael's feet climbing above her head, she started up the ladder. Menowski's grunt echoed through the shaft as he followed them.

Nato stopped twenty feet up the ladder at the steel bulkhead that sealed level two of the shaft. "Hold up. I'm opening the bulkhead." Holding the ladder with one hand, Nato wound the locking handle on the hatch over his head. When the locking bolts had retracted, he pushed it up. Sea water started to pour in, and Nato heaved the hatch open until it clanged against the steel wall.

"Keep going!" Nato yelled over the noise of the waterfall.

The convoy resumed the climb as the flow of water eased and dripped around them. Menowski waited impatiently for the chick to start moving. The ladder vibrated, and a low moaning sound rippled up the shaft.

"What the fuck was that?" Michael asked.

"Nato," Menowski called, the warning clear in his voice. "We've got infected coming out of the water."

"Are they climbing up?" Nicole asked, trying to look down past Menowski's broad shoulders and heavy load.

"No, they've grown wings and are flying up my fuckin' ass," he replied.

"Move it!" Nato shouted. He started double-timing up the ladder, his light dancing wildly as he scrambled up the rungs.

"Nicole! Climb past me!" Michael pressed himself to one side of the shaft and waited while Nicole hurried past.

"Get moving, squint!" Menowski was coming up fast and had no time for Michael to play hero.

"I'm at the escape hatch!" Nato yelled. He spun the handle and pushed the door open. The round tunnel sloped downwards, like a dry waterslide heading towards an unseen destination.

Grabbing the rail over the hatch, Nato went in feet first and threw himself down the slope. Lifting his legs, he built up speed, sweeping around the curves and trying to see what was coming up.

A few seconds later, he hit open air, then bounced into a trampoline-like net and rolled off onto the concrete floor of a small room.

"It's okay!" he yelled up the pipe. Nicole shot out of the tunnel, screaming as she flew into the air and then bounced on the net.

Nato grabbed her and dragged her aside. A few seconds later, Michael came cannoning out of the slide and hit the net with a grunt.

"Whoa!" he said, rolling off and dropping to the floor.

Gunfire echoed down the tunnel. The three of them stood staring up into the dark pipe. Flashes of light cast eerie shadows, and Menowski seemed to be hunkered down in the shaft, firing at the infected as they crawled up the ladder.

"Menowski!" Nato yelled up the tunnel. "What the fuck are you doing?"

"Get out of here, Nato; I'll be right behind you!" Menowski shouted, the steady clack of him reloading punctuating his words.

"Do not make me come up there and beat your ass, Marine!" Nato roared.

Michael went to the mini-sub. It was a tiny ship of thick steel with tiny portholes of armored glass. It looked like the remote craft used to explore the deepest channels of the trench, except this one had been stripped of all the scientific equipment they often carried.

Michael opened the hatch and peered inside. Exploration submersibles were Spartan on the inside at the best of times; this one looked like an empty tin can with a single set of drive controls and a radio set bolted to the wall. There were no seats, but he saw heating coils running around the inside that would keep them from freezing to death too quickly.

"Is it okay?" Nicole asked.

"Yeah. We need to get in, flood this chamber, and open that door." Michael jerked his head towards the large steel hatch in the floor.

Nicole stepped back and looked up. The mini-sub was secured by a chain on some kind of hook. It looked like it could be released from inside the sub.

Michael jumped down. "Get in the sub. I'll find the hatch

controls."

"There's a hook on the top of the sub; it should release inside. You know, like a glider disconnecting from a tow plane?"

"I can't say I have ever had the chance to try gliding."

Nicole shook her head and climbed up into the sub. She flicked the clearly marked switches on the control console and was relieved to see the batteries showed full charge. The sub was simple to operate, as if they expected it to be piloted by someone who had no experience.

"Menowski!" Nato yelled again. The gunfire continued and then went silent. Nato raised his rifle and covered the opening of the escape tunnel. He tensed but did not fire when Menowski's boots appeared, quickly followed by the rest of the marine.

"You're late," Nato said, extending a hand and pulling Menowski to his feet.

"One of them was the Sarge," Menowski said. "I put him out of his suffering."

"Ooh rah," Nato said. "Get on the sub, and make sure that fucking civilian is onboard."

Menowski strode over to where Michael was trying to make sense of the room's hatch and pump controls.

"Get on the sub," he ordered.

"I've almost got it!" Michael replied.

Menowski grabbed the smaller man by the shoulder and bodily moved him to the sub. "Get in there, or I will shoot you myself."

Michael scrambled into the sub, taking a seat against the wall next to Nicole. The rucksacks with the sealed specimen containers between their knees.

"Nato! Once I set the hatch to open, this room is going to flood and the sub can drop out through the floor. We're either on it or we set a new free-dive record for about three seconds!"

Nato was still focused on the dark entrance to the tunnel they had slid down. "I'll take care of it. Get on board!"

Menowski hesitated until Nato turned and glared at him. "I said, get on board!"

The marine scrambled up to the submarine hatch and crawled inside. With a professional confidence, he checked the systems and made the sub ready to fly as soon as they were in the water.

Nato backed away from the tunnel, the wet slapping sounds and gurgling groans coming down the pipe filling him with unease. He twisted the levers and pressed the emergency evacuation button on the wall panel. A klaxon sounded and lights flashed. He turned and headed for the sub. The hatch would open slowly, giving him plenty of time to get on board and secure the hatch.

Water started pouring down the escape tunnel, and in the flow, a grey-skinned figure slid out of the pipe and clawed its way off the safety net. Nato opened fire, shooting the squirming thing until its head came apart and the body lay still. Others came down the pipe, landing with wet splats on the remains of the first infected.

Nato kept shooting as the net filled with a deadly catch. He stepped on to the sub and fired the last of his magazine into the crawling mass of infected dropping onto the concrete floor.

Sliding into the sub, Nato pulled the hatch closed and locked it tight.

"Everyone okay?" he asked.

They nodded and moved closer together to make room for Nato in the cramped space.

"We'll be out of here soon."

The metal submarine vibrated as the hatch under them opened and water roared up, flooding the room.

Dull slapping sounds reached them as the infected banged on the shell of the sub. Nicole tried not to flinch, reminding herself that they were safe in here, and in a few minutes, they would be on their way home.

The acoustics of the chamber changed as the room filled with freezing sea water.

"Anytime you're ready, Menowski," Nato said.

"Hold on to your asses," Menowski replied and pulled the cable release handle above his head. Nothing happened. He pulled it again. Still nothing.

"You can jerk off on your own time..." Nato growled.

"Let it go, you fuckin' sonnovabitch..." Menowski tugged on the handle a third time. The sub jerked as the cable released and they dropped into the water.

CHAPTER 21

"Fucking drive straight!" Nato said.

Menowski's grip on the controls was white-knuckled as the sub bounced off the rock walls of the flooded tunnel and he over-corrected.

The flow of water was pushing them out. The flooding of the sub chamber had completed, and they were using the small propellers of the submarine to move under power.

"I see darkness!" Nicole shouted.

"What?" Menowski jerked his head and then went back to staring through the pilot's porthole.

"Darkness, that means open ocean!" Nicole explained.

"Few more feet... Just a few more feet..." Menowski seemed to breathe again as the sub burst out into the dark water.

Nato snatched the handset of the radio from its cradle. "Ishmael, Ishmael, this is fire-team Beta. Do you copy?"

"Copy, Beta Team, this is Ishmael. What is your sit-rep, over?"

"Ishmael, we have data and specimens of agent. Mission accomplished. We're in an escape sub and require immediate evac, over."

"Confirmed, Beta Team. We have you on sonar. ETA your position five minutes."

"Copy that, Ishmael, look forward to seeing you." Nato let his hands drop into his lap. "Sub'll pick us up in a few minutes."

Michael breathed, letting the tension flow out of his shoulders and letting his thoughts settle for the first time in days. He glanced at Nicole. She was pale under her tan, staring at the cold steel floor, her knees drawn up to her chest.

Michael hoped that they would have the opportunity to laugh about all this one day. He had a moment of hope that blessed day would include a few tropical cocktails at a resort somewhere. Maybe with a pool, instead of a beach though.

The sub boomed, and a violent shock threw Michael across the cabin and against Nicole. Nato crashed against them both, and Menowski slammed into the curved steel wall.

"We hit something?" Michael said, his voice muffled by Nato's arm pressing against his face.

The sub rolled again, the controls jerking as the rudders tilted wildly. Crawling into a more comfortable position, Nato checked on Menowski. The pilot had been knocked unconscious, a trickle of blood running across the bridge of his nose.

"Saint-Clair, okay?" Nato asked.

"I'm fine, but guys... you might want to see this."

Nicole pulled back from the porthole she had been pressed against. A pale shape slithered across the glass and then slammed into the hull with enough force to knock them sideways again.

"It's the infected," Nato said.

"No," Nicole shook her head. "It's Gretchen. Her metamorphosis is complete."

The radio crackled with the voice of the nuclear submarine comms officer. *Beta Team, Beta Team. This is Ishmael, do you copy?"*

Nato grabbed the handset. "Beta Team, receiving, over."

"We're getting some strange sonar readings on your position. Do you see anything, over?"

"Affirmative, Ishmael. We've got a giant jellyfish trying to get in and eat our brains, over."

The radio was silent for a moment. *"Beta Team, this is Ishmael, repeat your last, over."*

"Advise extreme caution during docking and rescue op," Nato said to the radio. "Hostile predator is attacking our vessel, over."

"Roger, Beta Team. Preparing for emergency docking and transfer of personnel."

The loud ping of active sonar rippled through the tiny submarine, and a moment later, the scraping sound of a steel hull brushing against theirs.

"You two, secure Menowski. I'll put us in position for hatch-to-hatch transfer."

Nicole and Michael dragged Menowski across their laps and held him steady as the tiny submarine dipped and twisted. The giant creature outside curled its translucent tentacles around the hatch-locking ring and contracted its body in one massive muscular spasm. The steel hull creaked and groaned under the strain.

Nato pulled back on the controls, driving the sub up against the curving black underbelly of the much larger nuclear submarine. The impact ground the beast between the steel hulls, shredding the gel-like flesh and forcing it to release its grip. The thing retreated, leaving chunks of itself caught on the hatch of the smaller sub.

On the underside of the nuclear vessel, a hatch opened, and the smaller sub rose until the two docking rings came together. Electric motors whirred and locked the two vessels together, like a remora clinging to a much larger shark.

"Beta team, this is Ishmael. Systems show secure connection. You can open your hatch and disembark your vessel."

Nato didn't bother replying. He rose up on his knees and twisted the locks open on the inside of the hatch. A little water splashed down, along with a large chunk of translucent jelly.

"Up and out!" Nato ordered. "Saint-Clair, you go first. There'll be people on the other side to help you. Go!"

Nicole scrambled out of the hatch. Hands reached down and grabbed her arms, lifting her up and pulling her to one side. She saw faces in NBC containment suits. Full gasmasks, head-to-toe protection, and thick gloves.

"We're not infected!" she insisted.

Menowski's limp form was lifted up through the narrow hatchway. The biohazard-protected crew took him and immediately laid him out in a clear plastic body bag which was sealed.

Michael came up out of the hatch and was immediately taken into secure custody.

"That fucking thing is coming back!" he yelled. "We need to get out of here!"

Nato reached up through the open hatch as the submarine around him shuddered, and with a shrieking of metal, the small vessel was sheared off the docking ring. High-pressure jets of water immediately burst in through the millimeter gap, slicing through Nato's arms and neck like a high-powered laser. The spray turned crimson and the air filled with the stink of salt water and blood.

The crew evacuated the airlock, knocking Michael down and dragging him out of the tight space that was rapidly flooding with water.

Menowski was left behind as they sealed the airlock, and a moment later, the exterior hatch also closed.

"Breach contained!" one of the crew shouted through his gasmask. "Get these people into secure quarantine!"

Nicole struggled against their grip, screaming she wasn't infected. Michael was shaking his head, saying something she couldn't make out as they slid a body-length plastic shroud over his head and secured him in it. The smell of disinfectant filled her nostrils, and the same kind of heavy-duty plastic bag swept over her as well.

Nicole struggled, trying to breathe, trying to break free. *This wasn't right. They weren't infected!* She clawed at the plastic with her fingers as the entire bag was lifted and she was carried down a narrow corridor.

Her hands caught the light shining down from the close ceiling, and she froze. For a moment, her skin shimmered with a silver translucence, and she felt something alien start to move in her flesh...

THE END

CHECK OUT OTHER GREAT
DEEP SEA THRILLERS

PREHISTORIC BEASTS AND WHERE TO FIGHT THEM
by Hugo Navikov

IN THE DEPTHS, SOMETHING WAITS...

Acclaimed film director Jake Bentneus pilots a custom submersible to the bottom of Challenger Deep in the Pacific, the deepest point of any ocean of Earth. But something lurks at the hot hydrothermal vents, a creature—a dinosaur—too big to exist.

Gigadon.

It not only exists, but it follows him, hungrily, back to the surface. Later, a barely living Bentneus offers a $1 billion prize to anyone who can find and kill the monster. His best bet is renowned ichthyopaleontologist Sean Muir, who had predicted adapted dinosaurs lived at the bottom of the ocean.

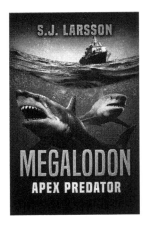

MEGALODON: APEX PREDATOR
by S.J. Larsson

English adventurer Sir Jeffery Mallory charters a ship for a top secret expedition to Antarctica. What starts out as a search and capture mission soon turns into a terrifying fight for survival as the crew come face to face with the fiercest ocean predator to have ever existed- Carcharodon Megalodon. Alone and with no hope of rescue the crew will need all their resources if they are to survive not only a 60 foot shark but also the harsh Antarctic conditions. Megalodon: Apex Predator is a deep-sea adventure filled with action, twists and savage prehistoric sharks.

CHECK OUT OTHER GREAT DEEP SEA THRILLERS

HELL'S TEETH
by Paul Mannering

In the cold South Pacific waters off the coast of New Zealand, a team of divers and scientists are preparing for three days in a specially designed habitat 1300 feet below the surface.

In this alien and savage world, the mysterious great white sharks gather to hunt and to breed.

When the dive team's only link to the surface is destroyed, they find themselves in a desperate battle for survival. With the air running out, and no hope of rescue, they must use their wits to survive against sharks, each other, and a terrifying nightmare of legend.

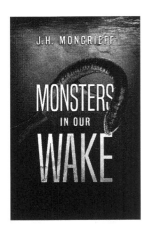

MONSTERS IN OUR WAKE
by J.H. Moncrieff

In the idyllic waters of the South Pacific lurks a dangerous and insatiable predator; a monster whose bloodlust and greed threatens the very survival of our planet...the oil industry. Thousands of miles from the nearest human settlement, deep on the ocean floor, ancient creatures have lived peacefully for millennia. But when an oil drill bursts through their lair, Nøkken attacks, damaging the drilling ship's engine and trapping the desperate crew. The longer the humans remain in Nøkken's territory, struggling to repair their ailing ship, the more confrontations occur between the two species. When the death toll rises, the crew turns on each other, and marine geologist Flora Duchovney realizes the scariest monsters aren't below the surface.

CHECK OUT OTHER GREAT
DEEP SEA THRILLERS

LOCH NESS REVENGE
by Hunter Shea

Deep in the murky waters of Loch Ness, the creature known as Nessie has returned. Twins Natalie and Austin McQueen watched in horror as their parents were devoured by the world's most infamous lake monster. Two decades later, it's their turn to hunt the legend. But what lurks in the Loch is not what they expected. Nessie is devouring everything in and around the Loch, and it's not alone. Hell has come to the Scottish Highlands. In a fierce battle between man and monster, the world may never be the same. Praise for THEY RISE : "Outrageous, balls to the wall...made me yearn for 3D glasses and a tub of popcorn, extra butter!" – The Eyes of Madness "A fast-paced, gore-heavy splatter fest of sharksploitation." The Werd "A rocket paced horror story. I enjoyed the hell out of this book." Shotgun Logic Reviews

TERROR FROM THE DEEP
by Alex Laybourne

When deep sea seismic activity cracks open a world hidden for millions of years, terrifying leviathans of the deep are unleashed to rampage off the coast of Mexico. Trapped on an island resort, MMA fighter Troy Deane leads a small group of survivors in the fight of their lives against pre-historic beasts long thought extinct. The terror from the deep has awoken, and it will take everything they have to conquer it.

Printed in Great Britain
by Amazon

28637036R00085